'Written in blood, directed by a deft hand and an intrepid mind, Mella's fearless yet precise prose is scintillatingly immediate and protean. Haunted it may be, yet *Older Brother* is very much alive and kicking. In fact this slim and vital novel is a tour de force; it will floor you, and lift you right the way up - I adored it.'
Claire-Louise Bennett, author of POND

'Mella's (…) work is not unlike his great coåmpatriot Juan Carlos Onetti. It demonstrates why he's among the most promising authors on the continent.'
Leo Boix, *Morning Star*

'Mella is an ambitious intellectual, drawn to big themes like grief, love, nihilism, and both individual and social violence. Thus, *Older Brother* is as much a philosophical think-piece as it is an absorbing, often touching tale of fear and loss. But do not be daunted, this is a truly rewarding read, rich with insight, humanity and a stirring beauty.'
The Big Issue

'*Older Brother* is one of those books that with time will become essential, being as harsh as it is luminous. It delves into the very necessary territory of that which is not usually spoken about.'
El País (Spain)

'Mella throws the torch onto the floor and sets fire to his house. He dives to the bottom of his basic instincts, his sex life, his family affairs and above all, his mind. It is a book of self-questioning, of psychoanalysis without a therapist.'
Mauro Libertella, Bogotá39 author

'A must-read novel. (...) This is a cathartic novel, another step in the consolidation of Mella as a remarkable writer.'
El País (Spain)

'*Older Brother* is an extraordinary novel that describes the calamity of a family in the aftermath of their son's death'.
Andrés Ricciardulli, *El Observador* (Uruguay)

WINNER of the **BARTOLOMÉ HIDALGO PRIZE** 2017

OLDER
BROTHER

CHARCO PRESS

First published by Charco Press 2018
Charco Press Ltd., Office 59, 44-46 Morningside Road, Edinburgh
EH10 4BF

A CIP catalogue record for this book is available from the British
Library.

ISBN: 9781999859343
e-book: 9781999859398

www.charcopress.com

Edited by Robin Myers
Cover design by Pablo Font
Typeset by Laura Jones
Proofread by Charlotte Coombe & Ellen Jones

2   4   6   8   10   9   7   5   3

Daniel Mella

OLDER
BROTHER

Translated by
Megan McDowell

CHARCO PRESS

AUTHOR'S NOTE

Some readers will pick a book from the shelf, read the first line and decide if it's good or not. Others, the minority, will go directly to the end and read the last line or the last paragraph to determine whether the book is worth their money. I am the first kind of reader. When I pick a book from the shelf, I read the first line to see if the author sucks or not. Since I am occasionally also a writer, I pay special attention to my first lines, to my beginnings. I also love a good ending, of course, but I would never pick up a book in a bookshop and read the final lines. I'd rather leave it as a surprise. I trust that a writer capable of writing a good beginning will also be capable of writing a good ending, although naturally that is not always the case. If you are one of these two kinds of readers, no doubt you've already decided to buy this book. And I thank you for that.

Curiously enough, the book you're about to read deals with beginnings and endings (although maybe that's what all books are about). Birth and death, the end of love and the beginning of insignificance, and so on, and so forth. It is also a book that has earned me a lot of comments, from people who know me well and from people who know me barely at all. These could be summed up along the following lines: that I had spent all my life waiting to write this book, that everything I had written before was a mere preparation for this novel, and that from now on it will be hard for me to write something better unless I reinvent myself. A close friend of mine was the one who made this last remark. She has faith in me. She says I've always known how to reinvent myself. I want to believe her more than anything in the world. And I'm working on it.

Daniel Mella
Parque del Plata, Uruguay
November 2019

For my family: without you, there would be no story.

His death will fall on 9th February, always two days before my birthday. Alejandro will be thirty-one years old in the early morning of that day whose light he will never see, the day we'll go from being four siblings to three. I, the oldest son, will be about to turn thirty-eight. That same morning, Mum (sixty-four), sitting beside me in dark glasses, says: 'Why him, when he liked life so much? Why Ale, when so many other people go around complaining about things all the time?'

On the back porch of my parents' house, while Dad (sixty-nine) and Marcos (twenty-seven) are on their way to Playa Grande to identify the body, I brew *mate* for the guests: the cousins, the aunts and uncles, several neighbours. Since no one sits still I have trouble remembering the order the gourd should be passed around in. Mum wasn't far off the mark.

You're right, I tell her. It should have been me.

She huffs. She didn't mean that. But I tell her that it would have been entirely fitting. Right? After all, who's the pessimist around here? I ask her.

'Why does everything always have to be about you? The truth is, I don't know what's got into you lately. You were better, but lately I just don't know.'

I ask her when the last time she saw me happy was. But happy like Alejandro, I say: bursting with happiness. Every stew he ate was the best stew he'd ever had, remember? If he rode a wave, it was the best wave of his life. Have you ever seen me completely happy?

Mum looks at me for a few seconds. I can't see her eyes behind the glasses. Her hands are resting on her knees and her foot taps a nervous rhythm.

'I can't think right now,' she says.

Because it's not easy to remember, I tell her. But when was the last time you saw Alejandro happy? I'm sure Ale was happy the last time you saw him. And the time before that, too, and the time before that... Wasn't he the happiest guy you knew?

'Yes and no. I always thought that Ale had a sadness deep inside him. The life he led, no commitments...'

But who doesn't have that? Who isn't always a little sad, deep down? Really, though, you can't argue that Alejandro wasn't the best equipped for life out of all of us. Who else had those shoulders? You remember how broad his chest was? He was a lion. He was solar.

'I remember his hugs. I remember how he used to call me Mumsy,' says Mum.

Everyone remembered his hugs. Alejandro hugged everyone. He liked to wrap you in the immensity of his body. He did it to show off. He'd hug you so you'd feel his muscles. He'd hug you till you felt the bulge through his trousers.

Once, when I was four years old, I'd knelt down beside my mother's bed where she lay with the flu, and I'd started to pray for her to get well. She likes to say that it made her feel better immediately. It's one of her classic memories of me. I always liked to hear her recall that moment, even during our most difficult times. She told that story so often – was she asking me, in a way, to never stop praying for her? I'd never known how to help her. She had never asked me for help. As far as I knew, she'd never asked anyone for help.

2

She doesn't like *mate*. I pass her one anyway. When she finds herself holding the gourd she hands it back to me, gets up, and goes inside without another word, pulling the sliding glass door behind her.

It's always the happiest and most talented who die young. People who die young are always the happiest of all, I announce to Aunt Laura as soon as Mum is gone.

My aunt, in a chair to my right, has heard our whole conversation. She's my father's only sibling. Just like Dad's, just like mine, her spine is fucked. Our backs are all broken in the lower part. Mine was a vertebra in the sacrum. What you see in an X-ray of my sacrum is a face of translucent bone, its eyes empty — a being from another planet. Chinese doctors call it the face of God. The nose is wide and long and full of protuberances. The mouth, a slightly forked crack, evokes the closed lips of certain reptiles.

Don't you think? I ask her. The happiest or the most talented. It's like a law, isn't it, Aunt Laura? You've got to keep an eye on the ones who go through life really happy. They're dangerous, right? They're always about to go to shit. I think about it with Paco (seven). With Juan (five), not so much. Juan is dryer, more ill-tempered. But Paco is a kid who wakes up happy, chattering away non-stop. He goes to bed happy, wakes up happy. Everyone will tell you what a cheerful kid, what a lovable child. I wish they'd stop talking like that. You can't imagine how afraid I am for Paco. Want a *mate*?

'You know what your brother told me the last time I saw him?' she asks me then. 'He said he had faith in that lifeguard hut.'

3

The last time she'd seen Alejandro was one night two weeks ago, in La Paloma. Dad was there too: he'd gone to spend a few days with her and my uncle, and it also ended up being the last time he would see Ale. That night they were going to make pizzas in the clay oven, and, knowing how much Ale liked them, they invited him too. He took the bus from Santa Teresa as soon as he left the beach. My aunt, who knew Alejandro was camping, had asked him where he slept during the storms they'd been having. He replied that he went to some friends' house on the other side of Cerro Rivero, but that sometimes he went to the lifeguard hut on Playa Grande.

'Can you believe it?' says my aunt. 'A lifeguard, a surfer, who knows very well how dangerous the beach is in an electrical storm. He said the hut had been there who knows how many years and nothing had ever happened to it, that it had made it through several winters without the wind tearing it down or lighting striking it. "I have faith in that hut," he told me.'

I didn't know Ale had said that. I never had minutes on my phone to call him. We texted, or he'd call me, and he had never mentioned taking shelter in the hut. Not once had it occurred to me that he could be in danger from the storms. I'd had other concerns that summer.

'I don't know if this time he didn't find out about the storm that was coming or what, but it's just horrible, don't you think?' she says.

He had faith in that hut. He left his body in a place he had faith in. I don't know if it's so horrible, I told her.

'I admire your tolerance for pain,' my aunt says then, using her thumbnails to wipe away her tears.

What do you mean, Aunt Laura? I ask her.

She sips the *mate*, nodding as she swallows.

'I admire you, really,' she says.

She doesn't know what she's saying, but it doesn't matter.

In the grass next to the wisteria, Enrique is drinking his own *mate* with Guido. Enrique is skinny, his cheeks sucked in by his missing molars. Guido has a potbelly and I've never seen him without a moustache. Ever since I can remember they've lived next door to each other and diagonal to my parents' house. Guido is still single fifteen years after his wife left him, he still drives a night taxi, and, at least on the outside, he makes sure to keep his house in good nick. The only difference between his house back then and his house now is the wall that separates it from the rat farm that is Enrique's house. The wall is over three metres high because Enrique, who swears he has a job sorting waste, has rubbish piled up in some monstrous structures made out of sticks and canvas. From the street there the rubbish heap appears to be completely haphazard. What you see is a bunch of canvases strung up over the piles of rubbish, and behind those you can barely catch a glimpse of the concrete block house built at the back, which was already in ruins when I was little.

'Don't those two hate each other?' asks Aunt Laura. 'Clearly, anything goes on a day like today.'

The morning of 9th February caught me at my parents' house. My sons were there, too. The day before, Monday the 8th, I'd brought them to visit their grandparents, and since their cousin Catalina (sixteen) – daughter of Mariela (thirty-nine) – was also there, we ended up camping out in the living room.

The first thing I hear when I come through the sliding door and into the kitchen is Mariela and the kids deciding what film to put on in the next room – my room, now my father's study. Mum, still in sunglasses, is on the sofa in front of the muted TV. She stares at the screen for long moments, then down at her hands in her lap. As soon as she sees me, she raises the right one, showing me her mobile phone in a strange gesture, as though in greeting, while she grips the remote control with the other hand.

'Could you send a message to Alejandro?' she asks me. 'I've been trying, but I can't see the keys.'

Alejandro's not there, I tell her. How could I possibly send him a message?

'Write: *Ale, tell me it's not you, Mum,*' she says. 'Maybe it's not him. Maybe they made a mistake.'

And then I'm kneeling before her and taking the phone from her hand, our heads practically at the same level. I explain to her, as though speaking to a deaf person, seeing myself reflected in the lenses of her dark glasses, that Ale's friends had called. It was Dwarf who found him, a guy who works with him, who sees him every day.

'If he was hit by lightning, maybe he was unrecognisable,' she says.

Just then, Mariela emerges from the hallway with the landline phone to her ear. She realises something strange is happening and she tells the person at the other end to hold on. She covers the mouthpiece and her yellow eyes bore into me.

Mum wants me to text Alejandro, I explain.

Mariela thinks for a moment, then tells me to send the message.

Text him? You want me to text Alejandro?

'Send it and it's done,' says Mariela, and she goes back the way she came. We hear her close the door to the master bedroom. On the porch, no one seems to be paying attention to us. Some of them have gone down to the grass to sit in the sun. Then it occurs to me that I could call him. I can call my brother and see who answers. I make the mistake of saying it out loud. Mum grows desperate.

'No!' she says. 'Don't call him, don't call him!'

Why not? We'll save time if I call him.

'Just send him the message, give me the phone, and forget about it, if it bothers you so much.'

But I won't be able to forget. I'll be just like her, waiting for someone to answer the message and hoping that whoever does is my brother, who no longer sees or hears, or has a voice, or fingers to work his iPhone.

'Text him and give me the phone, please,' says Mum.

As soon as I send the message, Mum takes the phone from my hands. She says: 'You didn't write what I told you to.'

I love you, cocksucker, I'd written.

'You think that's cute?' says Mum when she reads it.

Without warning, I feel the first tears of the day. With her silence, which I can practically lean against, Mum sounds out my pain, but my pain isn't mine. As if through divination, unable to prevent it, my mind forms the image of Alejandro still alive. There's no chance, but I picture him coming back from some girl's house, getting to work late, tired and hungover. Mum seems relieved that we're now drinking from the same miserable puddle.

'When we were outside,' she says then, delicately, 'I didn't mean that I would rather it were you instead of Alejandro. I would never say something like that. You misunderstood me.'

Don't worry. If there were ever a day to go crazy, it's this one.

She says she's going to take a minute and lie down.

Not long ago, in September, Mariela buried her baby daughter, Milena, so she knows exactly what needs to be done. She has all the numbers saved in her contacts, and she takes charge of making the necessary phone calls. Her partner Mauro, equally trained, offers his car to take Dad and Marcos to Rocha.

Sitting at the kitchen table, with the sound of the kids' film on the background, and Mum trying to sleep in her room, Mariela spells out the process: 'At the morgue they're going to open him up to see how he died. It was probably electrocution, but they have to rule out all the other possibilities. Tomorrow at eleven, the body will go to the Salhón funeral home, next to the shopping centre. We, the family, will have two hours to be with him there.'

She says it as though it had already happened.

'We're going to invite people to come from one to three. The procession leaves at three, and there will be a service at the same cemetery where we buried the baby. Whoever wants to say something will be able to. Instead of a burial, Dad and Marcos say Ale would have wanted to be cremated and to have his ashes thrown out on the beach.'

Thrown out?

'Is that OK with you? We'll take him to La Paloma and toss them there.'

It's OK, but you don't throw them out. You scatter them, return them, bequeath them.

I remember how the conversation was affecting my stomach. I remember burping and then saying: he died, he's dead. I remember repeating it. Then Mariela starts reheating the stroganoff. It was already close to noon and the kids hadn't eaten. As she looks through the fridge, cousin Timoteo taps on the sliding door, comes in carrying the thermos and asks us to boil more water. He hands the thermos to Mariela and goes back outside.

Mauro and Mariela waited fifteen years before they tried for a sibling for Catalina. Mariela wanted to finish university. Then do a postgraduate degree. Then the period when Mauro went on antidepressants after he lost his job. Then they separated for a time, Mauro living with his mother, Mariela teaching, researching and working on her doctorate. When Mauro was finally offered a job just like his old one at a new financial consulting firm, it was Mariela's turn to have a nervous breakdown, and she was forced to re-evaluate everything. She cut down on her work hours, discovered yoga, took up swimming again, and only then, after they'd got their stability back, did they start trying for the little boy Mauro always wanted. None of Mariela's examinations during the pregnancy revealed that the baby would be born without an immune system, due to a genetic failure that would also deprive her of all other normal reactions. They found out something was wrong only during the birth itself, when the baby didn't make any effort to be born and let Mariela do all the work. Milena couldn't latch onto the breast, her little fingers didn't grasp, she never returned a smile. But some communication was possible. I sang to her when I held her and her eyes stopped wandering. Sometimes you'd wonder if you were imagining it – and that doubt left you utterly alone – but the baby did listen. Sometimes she seemed to smile a sweet, crazy smile. Her temperature had to be taken every four hours, her oxygen had to be regulated, she received food and antibiotics through a tube. Mariela and Mauro personally carried out the nursing duties. During the nine marathon months of her daughter's life, Mariela's eyes turned yellow, forever changing from their usual honey colour.

'Idiot,' says Mariela while she fills the kettle with water. 'Going into the lifeguard hut during the worst storm.'

He had faith in the hut. Apparently he went there a lot. According to Aunt Laura, it wasn't the first time he'd spent the night there.

'I know, I talked to him. He didn't worry much about taking care of himself.'

He didn't give a shit.

'He didn't have kids. What was it Mum wanted?' she asks. 'For you to text him? Poor woman.'

After a few minutes of talking about who knows what, if we even talk at all, I ask Mariela if she doesn't think it should have been me who died instead of Alejandro. Mariela looks at me disconcertedly from the other end of the kitchen while she stirs the pot of chicken stroganoff.

I mean, if someone had told you one of us was going to die, who would you have bet on? I ask her. Wouldn't you have bet on me?

Mariela says she's never thought about it. Me neither, I tell her, but a second later I wasn't so sure.

I've always believed I'd be the first.

'And why would you think that?'

Because I'm the oldest?

'*I'm* the oldest.'

But she was a woman. Women don't count. Women live longer than men. Mariela shakes her head. She thinks it's very strange for me to think that way, as if these things followed some kind of logic. She thought I was smarter than that.

But it's not a question of intelligence, I think. Intelligent people were capable of believing the most ridiculous things. There was a time when I'd wanted to write about that, the idiocies dreamed up by people who are known for their superior intelligence. It was all based on what happened to Fernán, a friend of mine, a few years after he got married. The first thing he thought, when his wife didn't get pregnant, was that she was the problem. He thought of himself as a paragon of fertility just because he had a massive libido and was always ready to go. He thought the two things were synonymous. When the tests said he was the infertile one, he refused to believe it. He found it inconceivable. And he's one of the smartest people I know. Psychologist, journalist, essayist. I'm thinking about Fernán and about Bob Marley, Mariela's teenage hero who worshipped an Ethiopian torturer, when Timoteo comes back in asking for the water. Mariela had forgotten to put the kettle on the stove. She promises Timoteo she'll bring him the thermos as soon as it's ready. Then she asks me to go and ask Paco, Juan and Cata if they want to eat in the kitchen or in the other room while they watch the film. They unanimously come out in favour of the film. Then I lock myself in the bathroom to call La Negra.

At the end of December she'd moved the boys and her older daughter Yamila to Shangrilá, the neighbourhood where I'd grown up, to live with Fabricio, the fat guy she'd been dating for under two months. By some miracle, she answers my call. When I tell her the news, she cries: 'No! No! I can't believe it!' as if she and Ale had been close.

I ask her if she could come and pick up the boys: you think maybe you should come and get them? There are a lot of people in bad shape here, it's all really sad. Or maybe it doesn't matter, I don't know.

'What happened? What happened to Ale? What was it?'

Maybe it's OK for the boys to experience this. It's a death, nothing out of this world.

'Stop it. I'm on my way.'

Back in the dining room, Mariela is standing in front of the TV, and Marcos is on it, wearing dark glasses, his long hair pulled back into the same ponytail as always. He's carrying one of Alejandro's surfboards and has a bag slung over his shoulder. Dad, his silver head bobbing, walks in front of him. They're shown from a distance, walking between some low dunes. Maca (twenty-seven), Marcos's girlfriend, brings up the rear, carrying the other board. Mauro isn't in the shot; he must have gone ahead. Mariela is looking for the remote so she can turn up the volume. I tell her I'm going to let Mum know that Dad and Marcos are on TV, and Mariela tries to stop me.

'Why tell her?' she asks. 'Leave her be.'

Mum is waiting for Ale to respond to the text message. I find her on her side of the bed, sitting in front of the window that looks out on the street, the curtains drawn. She immediately gets up to come and see the TV. Mariela doesn't look at her at any point, doesn't see her freeze at the sight of the screen. Same shot, only now Dad, Marcos and Maca have stopped and are talking. Mum sits down in her recliner. While she settles her arms on the armrests, she becomes aware of the remote control in her left hand. She looks like she's about to use it, but she keeps the volume on mute until the end.

'I always thought one day I would see Ale playing guitar on TV. Not this,' she says, changing the channel.

'The water's ready,' she says later, when the kettle starts to whistle.

The kettle still shrilling, Mariela moving to take it off the stove, I get a text from La Negra: she's at the front door. I can see her behind the green bars of the front window, her head down, hands clasped over her belly.

'Are you going to let her in?' asks Mum, who can see her perfectly well from her seated position.

Instead, I open the door and go outside. La Negra

has done her hair in a hundred little braids. She follows me a few steps to the jacaranda tree, out of sight from the house.

'How are you? How is everybody?'

I need some air. I ask her to hug me. She does, quite deliberately resting her open palms on my shoulder blades. I can't remember the last time I had her so close. I try to smell her, but my eyes start searching for the fat bastard's white pickup; I can't help myself. I find it parked twenty metres up the street, pointed toward Giannattasio Avenue, the sun glinting off the glass. One of my hands comes to rest below her waist, where La Negra has a protrusion instead of a valley, the truncated tail from when she was an embryo. I tell her I'm sorry.

'What happened?' she replies, separating her ear from my chest, letting go of my shoulder blades, taking a step back.

I want her to forgive me for being an idiot. The calls, the messages, the invitations. I lost control. You don't know the hell I was in, I tell her.

'It didn't seem like love to me…'

My world was collapsing. Now I know it was nothing. This thing with Ale made me realise. It's over. The clouds have parted. Death is incredible.

'Apology accepted,' I hear her say, and I see her raise a hand to her heart.

On her way to the bus stop, a little girl with a backpack on, her hands stuffed into her jumper pocket, looks at all the cars parked in front of my parents' house: Mariela's, Leti's, my aunt and uncle's, the cousins', plus the white pickup. She must think it's a birthday, or a barbecue.

Her decision to stay with lard-arse Fabricio was for the best. She'd ensured herself a slave forever. Really, I tell La Negra, standing with her in front of my parents' house. He's solvent, he's got his own business. And he's not exactly good-looking; I mean, he won't turn many heads in the street. One less worry for you. You did well, good choice. If he's in the truck, tell him to come on over, it's all good.

'I came alone.'

There was a time when I'd even started praying. I'd got to the point of praying that La Negra would find someone, someone who would understand what went on in her head, who would love her the way she wanted to be loved.

'It's in the past, Dani. All that is behind us. What happened with Alejandro? Tell me. How are the boys?'

Ale was struck by lightning. The genius slept in the lifeguard hut and he copped it. There was a terrible storm in Rocha. I'll get the kids for you.

'I want to come in. If your mum is here, I want to see her.'

Mum greets her as soon as we come in. 'Brendita, I thought he was going to leave you out there.'

'Soledad, how awful!' says La Negra as they hug. 'How awful, how awful! It's all so sudden!'

'You're a mother, you understand me,' Mum says, sobbing like a child as La Negra wraps her arms around her and draws circles on her back with an open palm.

When the boys hear La Negra's voice, they come running from the bedroom and latch on to the hug between their mother and grandmother. I take that moment to go into the bedroom and get their things ready. Cata is lying on the bed and she asks me where Mariela is. I'm not sure where she's got to. I open the window to air out the room, scour the floor for the boys' socks, pick up their little trainers and put them in the backpack. Then I let a few minutes pass while I sit on the edge of the bed, watching *Pucca*, a Korean animation. When I leave the room, Cata has fallen asleep.

The goodbye goes quickly, though Mum, faithful to her habits, tries to drag it out by remembering at the last minute that she'd bought some little gifts for the kids. She goes to her room and comes back with a bag full of other, smaller bags that she pulls out and hands to La Negra.

'These are some little pyjamas I bought the other day, one pair for each of them. They can choose later,' she says. Then she takes out some educational toys and some mugs for their morning cocoa. 'I was going to take them to buy trainers today before lunch, but…'

Taking the large bag from her hands, La Negra puts the smaller ones back inside and hugs her one last time.

Juan runs to the truck as soon as we're out the door. Paco, though he starts off a second later, gets there before his brother. Wrapping her arm around my neck, La Negra tells me she cares about me a lot and she asks me to be strong, very strong. I want her to call me as soon as they get home so I can be sure they've got there all right, but she doesn't want to. How hard can it be? I ask her.

It's only five blocks, I need to calm down, there's no reason to think anything will happen to them. She's right. There's no reason for anything to happen to them, I tell her, but no one is ever free. There's never any certainty about anything.

'So you want me to call you?' she asks me.

For her to call me when they get home, that's all I'm asking. But she doesn't know if they're going straight home. Maybe she'll take them somewhere else first. Maybe they'll go and play on the swings for a while. The sun is nice. She asks me: 'You really want to wait who knows for how long to find out if we made it home safe and sound?'

Go straight home, I tell her. Don't go out, today of all days.

15

'I have to go straight home, I have to call you, what else?' she says, before shouting to the boys not to jump in the truck bed; they'd climbed into it without our noticing.

She doesn't have to call me. She can go wherever she wants. She's a free woman in a free country. Don't call me, I tell her. Don't let me manage your life. It's not that I'm nervous. I want to control you. No, I know what I want. It's something much sadder. I want my phone to ring, and I want it, for once, to be you.

'I don't know if you're being serious or not,' she says.

So don't call me, because I won't answer, I tell her. I haven't even got the words out before she shakes her head, takes two steps away, and then flashes me the exact same smile as she used to during our first days together, when she'd go with me to the bus stop early in the morning. She wouldn't wait for me to get on the bus. She'd turn to go as soon as the 6.30 Raincoop came around the corner, and she'd say *bye-bye* over her shoulder, smiling as she lifted her little skirt just a bit to flash me her panties all up in her arse, so I wouldn't forget what was waiting for me at home.

During the whole first year of our separation I never touched another woman. I wanted to keep them as far away from me as possible. I couldn't even look them in the eyes. I wasn't attracted to La Negra anymore. More than that – she disgusted me. And since she wasn't sleeping with anyone either, her body turned sad. She had a beautiful arse, but she started to lose it. I remember one time when I saw her from the window of a bus. It was almost noon and there she was, walking along the road dressed in white, on her way to pick up Paco and Juan from school. White trousers, white blouse, white leather boots, her hair straightened. The neighbourhood tart. She hadn't worn enough clothes, and her arms were crossed to keep herself warm. The trousers, which had once hugged the roundness of her buttocks, were now pinched and gathered. That's what you get for being a bitch. *Hija de puta,* I thought.

She was always dressed up when I went by her house to collect or drop off the boys. Sometimes that made me feel good, and other times it made me look down on her. I wasn't sure if she was trying to seduce me or show some dignity, and I wasn't interested in finding out. On Wednesdays I'd take the kids to school; on Fridays after school we'd all have lunch together at her house. We wanted the boys to see their mother and father sharing moments without friction, and we gave it our very best.

One of those afternoons after we'd eaten, La Negra handed me a *mate* and my fingers brushed against hers. I guess they always brushed hers, but that time I felt it. I felt the softness of her skin on my fingers. Starting then, we began to see each other during the school day. Some Saturdays she'd come to my house and we'd have dinner with the boys. The boys didn't know she'd stay over. So they wouldn't harbour false hopes, she'd get up at seven on Sunday and left before they woke up. We agreed that we weren't getting back together. We wanted each other; it was about indulging ourselves every once in a while, but we both had the freedom to be with anyone we wanted.

The sex with La Negra brought my testosterone back, and in a few months I was seeing Clara, a neighbour I'd run into at the bakery and the bus stop and who I'd previously only greeted with a hello or goodbye. On my way to the laundrette I'd go past her house, a little bungalow with a pitched roof and a bare front garden. On weekends I'd see her drinking *mate* there with some guy or a couple of girlfriends, listening to loud music, Extremoduro, La Polla Records, La Chancha Francisca. She had a broad waist that spilled over her trousers, which she didn't worry about hiding, and she had a beautiful face. To my astonishment she knew who I was, and she held me in high regard. She was twenty-nine and still needed to take a couple of exams to finish her literature degree from the Artigas Teachers Institute, and she'd been teaching for several years. She read a lot of Latin American literature, and she knew authors I'd never even heard of. Vargas Llosa and the Onetti who wrote long novels were her absolute idols. She was always re-reading them. In fact, she had moods when the only books she could only stand to read were *A Brief Life* or *Conversation in The Cathedral*. It had been a long time – over ten years – since I'd gone out with someone who had her own library.

When I stopped writing at twenty-four, I'd also left behind all of my literary relationships. La Negra didn't read, except for the occasional advanced self-help book (Deepak Chopra, Louise Hay) or some treatise on Chinese medicine, which was her line of work. She had a contempt for bookish people that suited me perfectly. Early on, she'd taken an interest in my books. She'd found them in the little library in my bedroom one of the first times she'd stayed over. She was leafing through them, sitting on the bed. I took them out of her hands. I forbade her to read them. They didn't represent me anymore. I was ashamed of them. I didn't even know why I kept them. They were a product of my depression. They're an affront to life, I think I even told her, and what we had between us was pure life. She was the first woman I was going to live with, and she was a mother, and I was in love, I felt positive for the first time in a long time.

In our first encounters she told me practically her entire love life. She'd started having sex very young, at thirteen, like it was a kind of game. In her family there was never a lot of fuss about bodies. Her father used to walk around the house in the buff like it was nothing. She'd always dated much older guys. She'd had two miscarriages, at sixteen and twenty-three, and she'd been in love with two men at the same time; they'd all lived together in Pajas Blancas. One of them had left on the verge of going crazy, and with the one who stayed, the one she'd soon have to leave, she'd had Yamila. I didn't ask for details about any of that. I didn't ask if the three of them slept together or if they took turns, and she didn't tell me. It was a boundary she set in her own story, to protect me, and it was for my own protection that I didn't cross it. I didn't have so much to tell, just that I'd debuted with a toothless whore in a brothel in Lautaro, in the south of Chile, on a trip I'd taken with the basketball team when I was seventeen. Before that, at fifteen, I'd sucked on my first little girlfriend's tits. Afterwards, I hadn't been able to sleep all night, and the next day I'd apologised for having disrespected her: this image summed up how pathetic my adolescence had been. Later, when I was older, I'd had two important girlfriends, but more than anything I'd dedicated myself to sex for pleasure, once I'd got past the dark initial phase of excess. La Negra didn't ask me what that excess had involved, and I didn't explain. My nocturnal, cocaine-fuelled excursions in Montevideo seemed too distant, and not simply because they were far in the past. Even at the time, they had already seemed far away. While they were happening, it was as if they were happening to someone else, and I'd never felt the need to share them with anyone. I also didn't tell La Negra about any of that because it revealed a sexuality that was sad and turbulent and superficial compared to hers.

It was only four years later, during the final period of our living together, when I'd found myself with the urge to take up writing again. I'd stay in the living room after dinner with a notebook, my tobacco and a thermos full of tea. It didn't take long for La Negra to start complaining. She didn't like it when I stayed up writing. To my utter shock, the reason – when I asked for one – was that sometimes Yamila got up at night to go to the bathroom. La Negra didn't want me to be there, didn't want me to see her daughter half asleep, in her underwear. Yamila was thirteen years old then. She was developing quickly, but she was still a child. I asked La Negra what she was afraid of. What did she think I was capable of doing to her daughter? She didn't reply with words. She looked at me with hatred and shame. I wasn't willing to stop writing, and again writing saved me, this time springing me from the cage of a relationship that had been collapsing for ages.

When I told La Negra I'd met someone, she didn't get upset. All she did was suggest I hold off on introducing her to the kids until I was one hundred per cent sure it was something serious. As it happened, I never did introduce them, though I considered it. A little surprised at herself, Clara went on the pill. She'd gone some time without a stable relationship and without any intention of having one. We didn't make any long-term plans, but we saw each other a lot. Clara would have liked to meet the boys, and I thought it could have a soothing effect on them; sometimes they worried because they thought I was lonely.

'Do you have fun when you're home alone?' they'd ask me.

During the first phase we'd slept together practically every night, at her house or mine. Wednesday morning, when we were both free, we'd walk to the estuary. Later on, when I was with La Negra – sometimes the very same day – I felt spacious, overflowing, unattainable. The more I fucked, the more I felt like fucking. I developed the shoulders of a gym rat. Now that I was on a roll, I also reclaimed the night. I returned to downtown Montevideo, to certain bars where friends had told me that my reputation had gained me a cult following. People remarked on how good I looked and asked me what my secret was. I told them the truth: sex, a lot of sex, and they laughed as if I'd cracked a joke.

Then, at the beginning of last December, just two months before Alejandro died, like an idiot I fell in love with La Negra all over again. All my desire, suddenly and exclusively, came to focus on her. The feeling was so strong that it forced me to end my relationship with Clara. Clara is going to look at me in utter surprise when I tell her what's happening to me. She'd had feelings for other people during all our time together, too, but it hadn't made her want to break things off with me. That's how couples work. For the first time in the past ten, almost eleven months, I sensed that Clara secretly hoped our relationship would work out. Something told me that by leaving her, I was closing the door to normalcy forever. Mornings with her were nice. Sex, coffee, reading the newspaper. When she saw there was nothing I could do to change my feelings, she swallowed her sadness. Somehow she always knew she stood to lose – after all, La Negra was the mother of my children.

'After all, she's the mother of my soul,' I would correct her, as if there was even the slightest possibility she would understand me.

The feeling will take me completely by surprise. It will gestate over four, five days and then attack me, leaving me utterly perplexed. One of the mornings when I go by early to take the boys to school, while we have breakfast and help them get dressed, La Negra won't draw out the moment when we hand off the *mate* in a caress. Then she's going to freeze when I brush her hip as she waits for the bread to toast. Then, when I tell her that after I drop the kids off at school I'll come back for a little visit with her, she'll reply that we'd better leave it for another time, today she's got some terrible premenstrual cramps. I'll call her later that same day to see how she is and to wish her good night.

The next day I'll send her a message telling her how much I miss her body and that I've had several ideas for our next encounter, a message she won't answer until the next morning. Thursday or Friday morning I again suggest a visit, but she's bleeding oceans and it's not like it was at the beginning; she doesn't let me touch her when she's on her period. On Saturday I invite her to come over at night, but Yamila (fifteen) is planning a party at the house with her school friends and La Negra has to be there. The next time I take Paco and Juan to school it will once again be impossible for us to meet: she has an appointment at the social security offices at ten. In each of her negatives I'll perceive a kind of deep-rooted regret, and I'm going to assume that La Negra is developing feelings for me, that she'd like to get back together and it hurts to have to share me with Clara, only she doesn't know how to tell me.

I will have already talked to Clara the morning when I catch La Negra in the kitchen and tell her how I feel. When I tell her I want to get back together, she will stiffen. I don't care how hard it's going to be to patch things up and forgive each other completely, I'll tell her.

I'm willing to talk for as many hours as we need to talk and to cover every possible point. She's going to look at me suspiciously. It's going to seem too radical to her. Love is radical, I'll reply.

'You broke up with Clara without knowing what was going on with me?'

I couldn't be with her anymore. Whether or not our relationship works, I don't want to touch another woman. I couldn't.

I'm going to insist. She'll ask for time. She needs to look inside herself, she has a lot of things to consider, it's all too sudden. When I tell her that I love her, she's going to peer at me as if there were something to interpret. I won't stop telling her, so she'll see how sure I am. I'll send her two or three messages a day: telling her about something nice I'm doing with the kids, or about something Paco did, something Juan said. Messages saying, *You remember the time when this or that?* and I'll get more and more enthusiastic. Every day that La Negra takes to reflect speaks to the seriousness of our situation, how open our wounds are, and I'm going to respect her caution. I'm going to prepare, I'm going to remember our story, searching for keys and clues that will help us repair everything that's broken. I'm going to regret, for starters, having relegated her to the role of a lover for all this time. I'm going to try to console myself with the idea that we've already gone through everything. What was left to us but to accept, once and for all, that life had put each of us in the other's path? I'm going to thank heaven for the renewed assault of this feeling, the sudden, luminous, poetic course of my life. I'm going to think of the boys' happiness; they're so little that they'll probably end up forgetting the couple of years when their parents were separated.

And one afternoon, burning with desire to see her,

I'm going to go by without calling first, at the time when she usually comes home after collecting the boys from school, and I'm going to find out that she's not there. Yamila will have picked up Paco and Juan and walked them home. It's Yamila who will be making some pasta for lunch. Apparently, her mother has had to go to Montevideo on some urgent errands and it's unclear when she'll be back. While Yamila finishes cooking lunch, I'm going to go outside with Paco and Juan to watch them ride their bikes around the triangular plaza across from the house. It will be a sunny, spring-like day, and my impatience will start to grow. It's almost time to go back to work and I don't like the idea of the boys being alone with only their sister looking after them, and I can't stop looking at my watch and staring at the end of the track where La Negra will have to appear after she gets off the bus.

Around that corner, eventually, comes a white pickup with its headlights on. At first I think it's a police truck. Some metres before it reaches the fork at the little plaza, the truck stops and sits motionless for several seconds. I don't know how I know, but La Negra is in that truck. I know that when she saw me in the street she asked the guy at the wheel to stop, and I know that she's just spent the night with that guy. She's explaining the situation to him; she's explaining who I am. Then, the pickup, in no hurry, turns onto her street and stops at the driveway. I cross the plaza to watch her get out of the passenger side: she meets my eyes as I walk. I look into the truck's open window, and I'm met by the stink of cigarettes and alcohol. Fabricio, a fat man with the look of a mechanic, introduces himself and shakes my hand, and then he says goodbye to La Negra. Talk later, he says.

At that moment, the boys will have dropped their bikes and come to greet their mother; they'll trail behind her as she goes in the front door without paying them the slightest attention. I'll wait for La Negra to come out of the bathroom while Yamila makes Paco and Juan eat.

Outside, as we sit in two plastic chairs, she's going to tell me about Fabricio with a cigarette in her hand. La Negra isn't a smoker. She smokes blonde rolling tobacco on special occasions, for short periods. She smoked when I met her. One cigarette could last her an eternity. She smoked it in deep concentration, taking pleasure from it but also, it seemed to me, as though consulting an oracle. That afternoon, after exhaling several mouthfuls of smoke, searching for the appropriate words, the proper tone, she'll tell me that with Fabricio she has the chance to experience something new. That's why she couldn't make up her mind whether to tell me about him, because of the newness and fragility of this thing she didn't know the name of, only that it isn't a silly love, a romantic love. Since I don't quite know what she means by that, she'll be forced to explain. I look at her mouth, and she sees me looking at it. She'd put on red lipstick in the bathroom, but it doesn't help at all. You can still tell where she was.

'What you feel for me is romantic love,' she'll say, covering her lips with her cigarette hand. 'It's not mature love. It's not real love.'

My vertigo will keep me from saying much. I can only ask her if she's already made the decision to stay with this Fabricio, if there isn't any chance she'll change her mind.

He was grey. La Negra was going to be with a fat grey guy. I go from sitting in my chair to kneeling on the ground. Then I slide down until I'm like a bracket against the wall. Then I gather the last of my strength to cross the dining room, and I end up stretched out on Juan's little bed.

I'm going to smoke more than I've ever smoked in my life during the weeks that follow, wondering what the fuck is happening. How can it be that I've lost her just when it seemed everything was miraculously falling into place? How can it be that after having lost her, my love for her doesn't diminish, but actually intensifies to levels I never would have thought possible? What evil spell has made me fall in love with her for the second time right as she's starting to go out with that fat arsehole?

I won't set foot in her house again during the few remaining days of school. The boys' holidays begin in the second half of December. She'll bring them to stay with me until Christmas, but she won't show up alone. She's going to come in Fabricio's truck with Fabricio, who's going to stay in the driver's seat with the engine running while I receive the kids in the doorway and she hands me a bag with their things. I'm going to call her several times while I'm with the boys, but La Negra isn't going to pick up or answer my messages no matter how long I wait, lying on the bed with the phone on my chest, checking it every once in a while even though it hasn't rung or vibrated. On Christmas Eve she's going to send a very short text wishing us a merry Christmas and letting me know that she'll come to collect them on the 27th. She'll stay silent when I reply, almost immediately, that we owe ourselves one last conversation, so we can lay all our cards on the table.

Paco is going to find me crying several times when he wakes up. He's going to ask me why I'm crying, then whether I'm crying for Mum. I'm going to tell him half the truth: that I'm crying for his mother and that he shouldn't worry, that I'll get over it.

I won't want to get over it. My love may be a childish love, it may be pure possessiveness, but it's untameable. It may be a bitter love, but it's also very sweet. The heart brought back to life after so long. The heart beating, flooded with an objectless love. I'm going to tend that love to keep it from waning. I'm going to worry about the day when that love will scatter like sand over the rest of the objects in the world. I'm going to try to silence my mind, which will teem with images of La Negra and fat Fabricio. I'm going to try. In the worst one, I see her having an orgasm and telling the fat muppet: *take it, take it.* That's what she used to say when she had an orgasm: take it. As if she were the one who was ejaculating. She must have said it to Yamila's father, too, and she must be saying it to the fat guy now. I don't think she inaugurated that habit with me. I never wanted to find out.

I'll also have images of us in old age, back together again, humiliated by time. Images of the two of us sitting there, remembering the past, reflecting on the winding path of our relationship. When I think that La Negra is an idiot for not returning my messages or calls, when I think about stopping by the fat bastard's house one day and beating the shit out of him in front of my kids, it's going to seem like those thoughts are of a lesser quality than the feelings my heart produces – feelings full of radiant energy. I'm going to feel split in two, mind and heart: the heart joyful, given over to its favourite activity, capable of limitless feeling; the mind irritated and at war. I'm going to tell myself that I have to trust my heart and give it free reign. I'm going to talk to my mind so it will submit to my heart. I'm going to tell it: Mind, stay in your place; Mind, don't be afraid.

Even though we don't have sex anymore, Clara still visits me. Now that the boys are on holiday and I have them with me, she texts before coming over. She'll come by at eleven at night, when Paco and Juan are already in bed. We go out back to smoke, sitting in the grass or on a couple of folding chairs. I tell her things I never told anyone about La Negra; I tell her about the jealousy that ate away at us, and she doesn't judge me or console me. She just clicks her tongue at certain moments of my story. A couple of times she's going to suggest that we sleep together, invoking the idea that one nail drives out another, and one of those times I accept. I let her suck me off there outside, under the stars. I look at her, and she's beautiful and feels splendid. She smiles at me, showing me that sensual gap between her front teeth, but she only gets me to half-mast.

'You're too cerebral,' she tells me after a while.

That night she stays over. Depressed by her presence in my bed, which is nothing but a symbol of La Negra's absence, I end up kicking her out in the early morning.

She and Alejandro are the only ones I talk to about the matter. With Alejandro when he calls from Santa Teresa on New Year's, which I'm going to spend at home. He's going to ask me about the boys and how things are going with Mum and Dad, who say I've been very aggressive lately, and I'm going to tell him about La Negra, who has just moved in with the fat wanker, in Shangrilá of all places, and I'm going to talk to him about the mind and the heart. Ale is going to ask me to be more patient with our parents, and he's going to say that the best thing that could have happened is for Brenda to find another guy, even if it doesn't seem that way now.

'Don't forget about everything that happened,' he'll tell me. 'Don't forget how badly you ended it. Remember how hard it was for you to get back on your feet.'

Then he'll tell me about the girls he's been hooking up with – five, though the season hasn't technically even started yet – and about a technique he's developed, the technique of dick rays and pussy rays. The technique consists of looking at the girl with your eyes but also with your dick. You have to feel like you've got a ray coming out of your dick that goes into the girl's pussy. It works. Even if the girl isn't looking at you, even if she's laying down sunbathing and looking in another direction, at some point she starts to feel it and she ends up turning toward you; and if the girl is into it, she starts sending you pussy rays. 'Really, I learned the technique from the girls', says Ale, 'from feeling their pussy rays while I was lifeguarding at the beach. Once it's established that there's a back and forth between dick rays and pussy rays, all the work is done. You go over to her, you say hi how's things, and you're good for the night.'

'Forget about Brenda,' he told me. 'And stop calling her La Negra. It's too intimate, you'll never be totally separated that way. And open a Facebook account, it's perfect for hooking up. Facebook is perfect for dick rays.'

Our last phone conversation will be on 6th January, which Ale is going to take off work so he can visit the family. No one knows, of course, but it will be the last time Alejandro sets foot in our parents' house. I'll be the only one who doesn't go – partly because of the heat, which means taking the kids on the bus will be absolute torture, and partly because I'll be too caught up with the problems in my personal life.

During that time, I'll be spending all my energy on finding some way to get the answers I need to keep me from exploding into a thousand pieces, or at least so that Paco and Juan's day-to-day isn't miserable, weighed down by their sad, exhausted, absent father. During that time I will have reached the conclusion that, at thirty-seven years old, I don't know myself in the slightest. Mine though they may be, I don't know what to do with my mind or my heart, each fighting a battle for itself alone. And my body: it bears up like a beaten animal under the tobacco and the insomnia and my erratic eating, but things can't go on like that forever. I always go to bed past three in the morning after masturbating to pornography in the living room, the computer's volume down as low as possible while the boys sleep on the other side of the wall. The page I always left for last had a category of videos starring amateur chicks, women of all ages willing to do anything for a little cash, faces worn down to the skull by poverty or addiction, and every video followed the same procedure. They started with the woman sitting on a torn sofa and the voice of a guy off-camera asking her what her name was, what she did for a living, how many guys she'd been with, if she liked to be fucked like an animal. At some point the guy would pretend to get bored with the protocol and he'd ask her to take her clothes off. While the girl undressed, the guy would tell her how ugly she was. They were ordinary women's bodies, most pretty run-down, with small or saggy breasts, paunchy stomachs, fat knees, cellulitis. The guy would criticise her arsehole, her legs, and he'd warn her she was going to feel like she'd been hit by a train. Then another guy would come out from behind the camera, his dick hard, arms tattooed, and he'd put the girl on her knees and start to mouth-fuck her. He'd grab her by the ears or the back of her neck with one hand and her throat with the other, and he'd give her one thrust after another while the other guy, who'd never appear, would encourage him to put it all in, to destroy her face. Sometimes, if the girl started to suffer and try to get away, a third guy would emerge to hold her arms behind her back. They'd let her breathe for a couple of seconds and the girl would pant, dripping slobber, her eyeliner all smeared. I'd go to sleep and have nightmares, Brenda's face mixing with the women's faces in the videos. I'd get up in the middle of the night feeling like I was going to vomit; I had a pain in the back of my neck that only lessened when I lay on my back with my legs up. One of those early mornings, I extracted a single thought from the tumult in my head: I need help. And then: I need to look where I haven't looked yet, I have to find some order in all this. And the next day I'll take Paco and Juan to the Tienda Inglesa so they can play in the ball pit and eat nuggets with chips and I'll go and buy a notebook. I'm going to start writing down my dreams.

The notebook, Papelaria brand, has a hard cover and a drawing of a woman on the front. Pale skin, almond eyes, her peacock-hued hair flows down the notebook's spine and spills onto the back cover. Although I quit pornography for good and cut down on my masturbation, the plan doesn't work immediately. The first nights I toss and turn in bed, smoking, looking at the notebook on the nightstand, going into the boys' room to make sure the mosquitos aren't biting them. Toward the end of the month, on 29th January, when I've already practically forgotten about the dream journal, I'll have my first dream. I'll get up right away to write it down: I'm at a party thrown by rich people, in a mansion, and I'm there because I won a raffle. I walk through the rooms, and people greet me with sardonic smiles. Finally, I manage to slip away. I go through some tall doors and find a crowd of people on the other side, some of them waiting to get in, others seemingly waiting for someone famous to come out so they can take a photo. No sooner do I get out the door than I'm being hugged by Ricardo, a friend I've barely seen for the past fifteen years, ever since he moved to Barcelona; he pulls me into his car. Ricardo had been my best friend when I was starting out as a writer. He was five years older than me, the same height as me but twice as wide and twice as agile, and when I met him he'd already published two unclassifiable books. They were a schizophrenic cocktail of Boris Vian, Lautrémont and Nick Cave, all mixed with a lot of whisky and insomniac nights, and a play he'd written had won a municipal prize. Where he was incredibly chaotic and garrulous, I, in comparison, was chaotic and silent. Ricardo had had a Dante-esque childhood and still had visions in the middle of the day, visions of rivers of blood and devastated cities. His apartment was a pigsty, the whole place littered with books, magazines and wrappers you had to clear away before you could sit and talk, and the bathroom was all sticky, but the guy, even with that impossible head of his, had taken care of himself since before he'd come of age, and I trusted him more than anyone. I still lived with my parents, and I'd just written *Mosh*, my first novel. After I'd abandoned Mormonism, the world had become so complex so quickly that for moments at a time I literally saw everything as a blur. Our conversations mainly consisted of Ricardo's monologues, which I received with rapt attention. Ricardo fed me information about what it meant to be an artist, to be a writer, to be a man. He lent me videos and detective novels. I was a personal project of his. He tried to orient me with his endless knowledge about art and artist myths, and he related episodes of his childhood and adolescence that were so much more extreme than mine, so much more explicit, and I absorbed his words, learned from his way of seeing things. He immediately became the first reader of my manuscripts. He almost always hit the nail on the head.

In the dream, his car is red and some of the bodywork is missing. You can see part of the motor and one of the doors is gone, but all of the brokenness is on purpose, like clothing that's intentionally ripped when you buy it.

Inside the car there's a boy and his father. The father is driving, the boy is riding in the passenger seat. The boy asks Ricardo, who is next to me, where he got the car. Before Ricardo can say anything, I interrupt him. I talk to Ricardo as if the boy can't hear me: tell him it's a fake car. Tell him I gave it to you, that my beloved's life is in danger. Meanwhile, we drive away from the party down a night-time street.

I'll find all kinds of meaning in the dream, but I don't study it deeply. It's enough that I'd had a dream in which Brenda didn't appear, and that I'd had the resolve to get up and write it down. I'll want to protect the energy that comes from this small success.

I'm going to dream again on the night of 30th January, again about a party, a kind of carnival I attend with a young girl who looks a lot like Natalia Oreiro. It's in the grounds of a school, with tables and chairs and benches. My brother Marcos is lying in the grass, talking to an Asian guy I've never seen, but they seem to have been friends for a long time. They don't see me, but I can hear them talking about my dream journal. The Asian guy says scornfully that he can only understand a person keeping a dream journal if he's writing about real dreams, not just any old dreams. It's growing dark and I lose sight of the girl I came with, and I find myself with a much older woman sitting on a swing. I sit beside her on the other swing. She's cold and I kiss her, and then I'm in a bathroom with showers; the woman from the swing gets in the shower with me. Meanwhile, I know that the girl is looking for me. She's a dancer and her show is about to start, and now her voice reaches me from somewhere, asking where I am. A security guard comes running into the bathroom, and as soon as he sees me, I've disappeared, I'm eating a sandwich in the middle of the playground, my hair dry, as if nothing had happened. It seems that I'm a famous actor, and people turn to look at me when I go into a warehouse set up for the show that features the girl I've come with. There's a net hanging halfway up to the ceiling, a tubular net like the ones they use to display balls at sporting goods stores, and a crowd of bodies squirm in it like worms; dancers walk over the bodies on their way to join them at the still empty end of the net. I can't find the girl, but some of the other dancers frown disapprovingly when they realise I'm looking for her. I go to a section of the stage that's like a house of mirrors where a thousand things are happening at once, and when I turn the corner I see her, or at least that's what my face expresses in the mirror; for a moment, that's the only thing I see – my face in the mirror. I turn the corner and see my profile, my actor's profile, my shoulders bare, and when I see the girl I smile in a way that tells me she still hasn't seen me.

In the dream I have on the night of 3rd February, I'm at my brother Marcos's wedding and everything goes badly. With a song by Creedence Clearwater Revival playing in the background, two naked men emerge from a pool, their dicks hard, and they stand there looking around at everyone and pointing their erections at us. My cousins and maternal uncles are disguised as Egyptians, apparently at my suggestion. My mother gets angry and some of them crouch down in the hallway, hiding their heads. Then I see Bernardo, who used to be my PE teacher in secondary school, and I avoid him by pretending I'm sleepwalking. There's an Indian actor who shoots at some glass walls that don't shatter when the bullets hit them. The rumour spreads that one of the guests at the party is a thief and is planning to steal something, but no one knows who it is or what he wants to steal, and we're all on guard. The Indian actor is leading the investigation and at a certain point he captures a young couple, who fight back. He wraps them in a kind of blue nylon bag that grows on its own and closes over the length of their bodies, like a cocoon.

The night of 8th February, a few hours before Alejandro returns to the nothing from whence he came, we'll have a long and wide-ranging conversation about survival – my dad, Marcos, Maca, Mariela, and Mauro. After ploughing through an order of mozzarella and *farinata*, we'll take our coffee out to the porch while Mum makes up the beds in what used to be my room. It might seem like a coincidence that we'd choose this very subject on the night Ale was going to die on us, but the truth is we always talked about survival when we got together, if my father was there: survival, the annihilation of the human race and the stupidity of the human species.

At first, it had always been Dad who insisted on starting those conversations. We ascribed it in part to the start of the new millennium, but especially to the fact that Dad was becoming a generic old man, seeing destruction and conspiracy everywhere he looked. Little by little, though, it seemed the world had decided to prove him right. After a while there was no need for anyone to even mention some disaster pulled from the pages of the news; we'd just launch straight into a rant against the Rockefellers and the Rothschilds and all the rest of the world's pricks. Bankers, masons, politicians, Zionists – no one was safe.

We can start off talking about anything, absolutely anything, but ultimately, we know it isn't going to last. Ultimately, we're waiting for the moment when the conversation will turn toward what really matters to us. And the end of the world matters to us, though we no longer seem able to treat it with complete seriousness. Or perhaps it's just that we no longer know exactly what to say or how to talk about it, as if we'd exhausted the subject but it still persisted, as if it always remained just a little out of our reach.

The conversation is always more or less the same. The variations, if any, are slight. If I remember certain details about this night in particular, it's because it was Alejandro's last night on the face of the earth. I don't remember how we started. I do remember that Mum sat with us for a while after she'd put the kids to bed, but when she saw we'd be complaining about everything for the umpteenth time she said goodnight, claiming to be very tired. I would have done the same, but I like the time after the boys go to sleep. Maca made *mate* even though it was after ten. It was the stormiest summer in years. That night's storm was the strongest of them all, though it only hit in the east. It would be a cool night for us, and, for once, clear.

I remember there'll be a warm breeze swirling in the garden when Mariela, talking about the project she's been working on at the Clemente Estable Research Institute, explains the function of a protein that transports an enzyme from one part of the cell to another. That will be one of the high points of the night. The protein's structure, in visual terms, is similar to a stick figure: it looks like it has two little legs at one end of the main filament and two little arms at the other. To illustrate the protein's movement Mariela will stand up, put her arms over her head like an aborigine carrying a basket and take some penguin steps.

I remember Dad taking that moment to apply his implacable logic: 'There's nothing for it. We're just so disconnected from nature,' he said. 'There you have that protein, going about its invisible business, not thinking too much. All in order to perpetuate life, so that nature can carry on along its course. That protein doesn't want to be anything other than what it is. It doesn't want to have more than anyone else and it isn't chasing any fame. It doesn't build machines to do everything for it so it can have more time to scratch its balls. But us? We go against everything, starting with our primary instinct. We destroy everything; we're on a suicide mission. Any other animal or any other plant would have realised it a long time ago. All creatures on the face of the earth are governed by the mandate of not dying.'

'Not dying?' Mariela will ask.

'Surviving, perpetuating themselves,' I remember Dad correcting himself. 'Isn't survival the first of all instincts? Well, we're the exception. We disobey it royally. And supposedly we're the peak, the most intelligent of all. Who sold us the idea that we're the apex? They ruined our lives with that idea. Explain it to me. We're the only animals that treat the gift of life with contempt. What other creature is capable of killing itself with drugs? We murder each other over football games. We kill ourselves for money. We risk our lives for a little adrenaline. There are people who voluntarily go to war. I can't understand it… What has to happen for us to realise that we're at the bottom of the bin? Is there any other creature that commits suicide, Mariela?'

'Dolphins can choose to stop breathing,' Marcos will say. 'When they're very depressed, in captivity for example, they can decide to stop breathing and they die. They're the only mammals with that control.'

Dolphins – beautiful, innocent, highly evolved dolphins with their suicidal exploits – will leave us stunned for a second of silence that, if I remember correctly, I will be the one to break, arguing that contempt for life may not be as negative as it seems. I will cite famous cases of scientists, inventors and artists who had forgotten to eat and sleep when they were working. Such people probably felt more alive in those moments than any other, I say. All the rest of it didn't mean anything to them. All the rest of it was just breathing, surviving, scraping by. A load of commonplaces, that's what our conversations are, but for some reason we need to say these things and say them again. What would have happened if Columbus had thought it was too risky to set sail for the Orient? I'll ask. Where would we be if Columbus had stayed home worrying about his little life?

'We'd be better off,' Dad will say, predictably.

'We wouldn't be here,' Marcos will correct him. 'We wouldn't know each other.'

As we later found out, by that point in the night Alejandro was already with Ana Laura, his girlfriend of the hour. He was the only lifeguard of the whole brigade who went home every night to a tent instead of a house – to keep costs down, so he could travel during the year. But that night he went to the hut; perhaps by that point Ale was already there, fucking away.

'I fear for my children's future. I fear for my grand-children's future. I think of Catalina, I think of Paco and Juan. I'm afraid they won't have a future,' says Dad, lowering his voice at the end, realising how depressing he's being.

That's the part of the conversation that I remember most vividly, because even though Dad is repeating something he's said a thousand times before, it's also true that he anticipates what's coming before anyone does. And later, before sunrise, at approximately the time when Ale's heart stops beating, Dad will have a formidable dream.

I am indignant that Dad is using my kids for hypothetical tragedies. He's been losing sleep over his holocaust images for years. Mineral holocaust, vegetal holocaust, animal holocaust, human holocaust. He thinks that one day the dictatorship will return, or something worse. He thinks that one day there will be a war over water, that people will come for it. When he goes to bed he sees warplanes, he sees tanks. He sees soldiers barging into our houses, he sees our neighbourhoods turned into Palestine.

He's a good man, my father. He plays with the boys, lets them collect snails in the garden, takes them to the beach, puts them on a surfboard the same way he did with us. I didn't have that kind of grandfather. But while he's with them there are moments – increasingly frequent – when a shadow crosses his face, and I know he's falling prey to those irresistible images. While his grandsons play, immersed in the present with perfect intensity, he imagines them inhabiting a planet descended into catastrophe, without clean air, without food. While they do a handstand or run after a ball, he's imagining them dead, raped in an all-out war, reduced to slaves.

On this particular occasion, because I don't want the thing to drag on much longer, I'm not going to react. I'm not going to ask Dad to leave my kids out of it. I'm not going to ask what it is he likes so much about those images, why he doesn't want to stop thinking about them. I'm going to sink into silence and hear Mauro say, paraphrasing the band Los Redondos, that the future arrived a while ago. And Mariela saying: whatever happens, if the world ends, it probably won't be how we imagine it. It won't be a meteorite or aliens. Then I hear her ask Dad if there was anything in his life that turned out the way he'd imagined.

'Is sex what you imagined? Old age? Work? Kids?'

Then I remember Dad asking Mariela if she's talking about Milena, and Mariela answering that she's talking about life.

'Is marriage how you imagined it would be?' she'll ask. 'Why would the end of the world be any different? When it happens for real, we'll have imagined it so much that we won't even notice.'

'This is the end of the world,' I remember Marcos saying then. 'No one's left alive at the end of the world. The end of the world is waiting for the end of the world.'

'For all practical purposes, it doesn't matter,' Mariela will say.

'Are you all still talking about the end of the world? How can you not get bored?' I remember Mum finally asking through the kitchen window, which looks directly onto where we're sitting. She'll say something else that we can't hear over the laughter, and she'll go back to bed with the glass of water she came for. In any case, the night won't last much longer. Since it's the same conversation we always have and there's no need to reach any conclusions, it's not strange for it to end abruptly. In fact, it usually ends up going slack, everyone exhausted. After helping with the dishes, Mariela and Mauro will go home, Marcos and Maca to the lair, and I'll settle in on the leather sofa in the living room. I won't remember anything I dream. I'll sleep more deeply than I have for a long time, and then I'll lie awake briefly as the sky starts to lighten, surprised by how good my body feels, when that sofa usually makes it suffer.

Apparently, they'd issued a magenta alert that night. It's the first thing Marcos mentions when he comes back from Playa Grande, after he drops Alejandro's bags on the floor in front of the darkened TV. Magenta: uncontrolled electrical activity. Marcos says that everyone – the neighbours, Dwarf, Canary, Worm, the police – said it had been like a bombardment during the night.

Dad leaves Alejandro's surfboards on the grass in the garden and then goes into a trance, his hands stuffed into the pockets of his Bermuda shorts. Mum goes over to him, takes him by the arm and leans against him. They embrace, awkwardly. She tries to lean into his chest and caress the nape of his neck, but he's too tall. Dad, trying to stay balanced, doesn't bend down far enough. Faced with the scene of my parents crying in the back garden, the people on the porch go into the dining room: Aunt Laura, Uncle Jaime, their daughter Leticia and cousins Ismael and Timoteo, who work together installing air conditioners and have cancelled their appointments. No one had heard anything about a magenta alert.

What colour is magenta? I ask. I direct the question at Marcos. He works in cinema; I figure he'll know. Marcos is sitting in Mum's chair and looking at Ale's bags. But he doesn't know. Some kind of red, he figures.

But is there anything in nature that's magenta? Or is it an artificial colour?

'What's strange is that Ale didn't know there was going to be a storm,' interrupts Aunt Laura then. 'Don't lifeguards get the weather report every day?'

She's asking Marcos, who also surfs and is always keeping an eye on the weather online while he writes his scripts and his movie reviews for specialised blogs. Marcos lives with Maca behind my parents' house, in the lair that Alejandro had built and lived in until less than a year ago. Marcos puts his elbows on his knees and doesn't answer.

'Do you think he knew about the storm that was coming…?' asks Aunt Laura. 'You don't all think he knew about the storm and went to the lifeguard hut anyway?'

Marcos isn't listening to her anymore. He seems out of it. He rocks harder and harder. Then I kneel down by one of the bags and ask him what we're going to do with Ale's things, and his eyes focus on me until he finally comprehends my question and stops moving.

We can't leave all this stuff here, I tell him.

The first things to appear when I open the bag are the Adidas trainers. They're a little small for me. Ale wore a forty-four, I'm a forty-five. They're made of a flexible fabric and they look good, more like dress shoes than trainers: blue with red designs on the sole, white stripes, white laces, and I'm in desperate need of clothes. Without private classes my income is cut in half in the summer, and since I spend most of the holidays with my kids I spend twice as much money, so I tend to look pretty shabby until March or April.

Ale's just saved me a hundred dollars.

Marcos extracts what look like construction boots from the other bag and he hands them to me along with the flannel shirt, which was folded. 'A hundred and fifty,' he says.

None of the clothes will fit him. Marcos is under five eleven, while Ale was almost six three. I had finally stopped growing, when I was sixteen, at six foot four.

'The bastard was huge,' says Marcos. 'You can't imagine how big that body was.'

It takes me a second to realise he's talking about Alejandro's corpse. Then a bubble forms around us. The others go on conjecturing about whether Ale had known about the storm or been caught by surprise. Every once in a while, one of them tries to look toward Marcos or me, but to no avail. I ask him where they went to see the body, and Marcos tells me it was in the prefecture and that it was enormous.

'He was huge. You have no idea how big he was.'

I would have liked to go and identify the body, but I wasn't about to leave Paco and Juan. Marcos says Ale wasn't too fucked up, just that his arm was contorted, the right one.

He didn't shit or piss himself?

'He'd only bit his lip, on the same side. His teeth went right through. You can tell that's the side that got hit.'

The hut wasn't destroyed. The lightning bolt had hit one of the iron posts that supported it. Right where the post went into the sand, it was bent and had a kind of gash.

In the last bag I go through, among a bunch of useless things, I found the books that Ale had brought for the summer. *Siddhartha* by Herman Hesse, *The Shadow of the Wind* by Carlos Ruiz Zafón, *Choke* by Chuck Palahniuk and *Lava*, my first book in thirteen years, which had been published a few months before. Alejandro had been with me while I wrote many pages of that book, during the first period after my separation, when I stayed in the lair. Ale practiced guitar; I wrote.

Lamp, the main character of the title story, which closes the book, is based on him. Or really he's based on Vispo, a friend from my father's youth. Athlete, inventor, composer, singer, jokester, womaniser, the life of every party. Dad used to tell us stories about him, and I was fascinated by my father's fascination. The kind of guy who other people can't help but talk about. The kind of person who someone, eventually, ends up writing about. The inspiration for Lamp was Vispo at first and later turned into Alejandro; then Uncle Antonio, my mother's alcoholic brother, found his way into the character. The charismatic types generally didn't write anything. Lamp went to the extreme of never even wanting to record one of his songs. He trusted that everything would be recorded. Everything left a mark, no matter how subtle. Lamp died at the end of the story. He was sick, he knew he was going to die, and he chose how he would go out. It was one of the things that for some reason had started obsessing me as soon as I broke up with Brenda. If someone was lucky enough to know he was dying, would he be able to plan out the moment itself? Would a person be capable of stage-managing his own death? Lamp, without the strength to go camping at Santa Teresa like he did religiously every summer, chose to pitch a tent behind his house in Jacinto Vera, and he spent his final days pretending he was out there among the pines.

After I drop Ale's bags in the computer room, I find Dad standing in the dining room. Mum, my aunt and Uncle, Leticia, Mariela and Mauro are all sitting at the table listening to him. Ismael and Timoteo have gone. Marcos is taking the guitars to the lair. When I come in Dad backs up a little, and now he's speaking for me, too. I was planning to boil some water for a cup of tea, but I stop in the doorway of the dining room and Dad repeats, for my ears, that going into the Santa Teresa prefecture had been like entering a time machine. It was the same as it had been forty years ago. The same walls, the same desk, or at least a very similar one; even the smell was the same.

'Fifty years, Miguel, not forty,' my uncle says. 'Fifty years, it's been.'

Along with Jaime, Vispo and another seven or eight friends, Dad was going to form a surfer group in the mid-1970s. His most intense memories are from that time: camping in Santa Teresa, the walks over Polonio's eternal dunes, guitar sessions around the bonfire. There was practically no surfing in these latitudes at the time, and, except for a few occasions when they met some Brazilian or Argentinian trying out our coasts, my father and his friends were the only ones in the water. They were explorers, they were pioneers. The expeditions would last at least ten or fifteen days, and they'd bring lard and flour to make fried dough, plus rice and onion and potatoes for stews, and they'd also fish and collect mussels.

'You remember the *milanesas* Alba would make for us?' says Jaime.

When they'd go to Santa Teresa, around the middle of their stay, when supplies were starting to dwindle or the guys were getting tired of the regime of stew and fried dough, Grandma Alba would surprise them, without fail, with several kilos of breaded veal filets sent through the mail.

'Mama's *milanesas*,' says Dad.

If this were a play, that would be the signal for Leticia to burst into tears. When your Uncle Miguel says 'Mama's *milanesas*,' just like that, *mama*, the way an Italian would say it, you, Leticia, can't take it anymore and you burst into tears.

Dad still hasn't taken off his bum-bag. His head is bowed, and he seems to be wondering what it is he's got tied around his waist.

'They had Ale in a box. In a tin coffin. The kind they use for everyone who dies on the beach. How was I going to know, forty-five years ago, that one day, in that same place, I was going to see my own son dead?'

I imagine him young, no more than twenty-four, younger than Alejandro, with the sensitive and serious face of his photographs, serious from a thirst for truth that was already starting to devour him. I picture him receiving the package sent by Grandma Alba in the prefecture of Santa Teresa. He isn't anyone's father yet. His love of the waves will eventually take him to Peru and Hawaii, all financed by his meagre salary from the Institute of Physical Education, and judging by how he'll tell his youthful stories later on, it seems it was the happiest time of his life. But when he feels himself overcome by the memories, his face will darken and he'll cut himself off, saying it was a selfish time devoted only to pleasure-seeking. It's a time that will come to an end when he meets Mum, at twenty-seven.

I think Leticia is also picturing Dad as young and joyful, but she's imagining that version of him here with us in the dining room, transported fifty years into the future, because Leti starts to cry more softly and she stares at him the way one might look at an innocent. Mariela, to my cousin's right, puts an arm around her shoulders. Then she retracts it and leans against Mauro. Mum is about to say something. She's looking at Dad, who hasn't taken his eyes off the ceiling, but when he does meet her eyes, she lowers them.

Marcos will give the news to my parents in the lair. He'll lead them out there from the kitchen, interrupting the preparation of chicken stroganoff, my sons' favourite food. He will ask them to sit down on the sofa. Mum will obey, Dad won't: he'll want to receive the news standing up, and he'll start to grow impatient. I don't remember what words Marcos will use. I'll be standing in the doorway; Macarena will have her arms crossed beside the stairs up to the loft. I will leave the scene in the middle to go and tell the boys what happened.

Paco, Juan and Cata will be drawing at the living room table. Catalina is going to curl up in the armchair to cry. Paco and Juan are going to look at each other, not understanding much, and then they'll look at me, seeking some indication of how they should feel. Juan, who loves superheroes and whom I've convinced that I am one, will tell me not to worry.

'Use your super-powers to make Uncle Ale stop being dead, and that's that.'

'This is the worst thing that could happen to us!' will be Mum's first cry from the lair.

'Fucking surfing!' will be the second. 'Fucking beach, fucking storm!'

I'll never know whether Dad heard her rue the day he taught us to ride a wave, because while she curses herself hoarse, he'll be leaning against the stairs that led to the loft, the bedroom of the lair, repeating: *no, no, Ale, what did you do?*

'Why did you ever teach them to surf?' Mum will demand. 'Why did you ever take them to the beach and teach them how?'

'Surfing has nothing to do with it, Mum…' Marcos will say. 'Ale loved surfing…'

'Surfing made him live like that! It's why he lived that petty life! A lifeguard! With all the potential he had! And why? To be close to the beach, to the girls! And now Alejandro is dead!' she'll cry.

'Don't say that, Mum,' Marcos will plead with her, on his knees, struggling to contain himself. 'Don't say those things…'

'Fucking storm! Fucking life!'

Several hours later, when Dad is talking about how time has collapsed, Mum will be about to throw the surfing in his face again; she looks at him enraged, entrenched behind the dining room table. It would be the worst moment for her to bring it up. But, sunk in a stupor, Dad beats her to it.

'It's my fault. Alejandro was living the life I didn't live. I left that life when I grew up,' he says. 'It's an empty life, but Ale didn't want children, he didn't want a partner. He wanted to be free. He was content with his music and the waves.'

And the girls, I say. He really liked the girls. He liked them all; how could he have wanted kids?

'Ale was woman-crazy, that's for sure...' says Dad.

'Well, he had what it took,' says Mauro.

'Those grey eyes,' says Mariela, taking the empty chair between Mum and Jaime. 'He was pure instinct.'

Pure instinct, but he didn't want kids. It's a bit weird, isn't it? I say.

'I don't know if it's that weird,' replies Mariela.

But he wasn't crazy for just any women. It was *hot* women he was crazy for. Alejandro went out with incredibly hot women. *Fit* women. You remember Agus? I ask. Stunning. Lucía? Stunning. But what were they? Silly little divas. You know what Alejandro has been calling girls lately? Ponies. I told him he could screw a thousand ponies, but you don't know what screwing really is until you have sex with a woman and you have sex to procreate. Now that's sex with all you've got. That's when you're really going for it. That's when you get the most out of sex.

Leticia runs out the door practically mewling. Aunt Laura follows her. They stand in the sun on the gravel path that leads to the lair, side by side.

'Could you watch your language a little?' says Mum.

I pour all the water into the ceramic thermos, then add two bags of black tea and a slice of lemon. Dad helps by bringing mugs and a jar of honey to the table. At some point Ale was going to meet a woman who would give

48

him children, I say then. It's true that he really liked sex, but at some point he was going to want to have a kid. If you like to surf, someday you're going to want to ride the most perfect wave, right? And the most perfect wave of screwing is screwing to procreate.

'So you talked to him about having kids too?' asks Dad. 'Who wants tea?'

I told him: hopefully someday you'll meet a woman who makes your head spin, and then you'll stop screwing around. That's what he needed. It's a rule. To be a real man you need a real woman. To stop being a kid you have to have kids, like it or not. Sure, there are exceptions, rare cases, but in the end that's just how it is; I don't care who you are.

Mum asks: 'Is that what Brenda is for you? A real woman?' and she slides her mug towards me. 'I don't want any tea.'

A person catches the wave of their life and it doesn't always turn out perfectly, I reply. Just ask Dad.

'It takes effort,' she declares. 'You have to make sacrifices.'

But the subject of this conversation was who killed whom, and we were digressing. We're digressing, I tell them. The question is, who's the killer. It can't be that Ale lived the way he wanted to. If he went into that hut on the beach in the middle of a storm, it has to be because someone made him do it. Maybe it was because his father put him on a surfboard once upon a time. But it can't be that he was simply struck by lightning and he died and that's it.

'This is the worst thing that could have happened to us,' says Mum, flushed red, pounding the table. She repeats it several times. 'This is the worst. The worst thing that can happen to anyone.'

Everyone averts their eyes and picks up their mugs to

keep their tea from spilling. Jaime looks toward Leticia and Aunt Laura. Marcos has joined them on the gravel pathway. He's standing in front of them and has a hand on Leti's shoulder. Mariela stands up and carries her cup of tea into the living room, where she stands stock still in front of the fireplace. The mantel displays photos of the whole family. The central photo is of Milena, lying on Mariela's chest, the oxygen tube cutting across her face.

'Why us, Miguel? Why us? It's unnatural,' says Mum.

Dad presses her hand down on the table. Mum tries to pull it away, but Dad doesn't let her. They wrestle for a while, in view of everyone, until Mum surrenders.

You don't know how terrified I am that Paco will die, I say then.

Mum asks me what I'm talking about and I say it again, but this time just for her. I say: it's not the same with Juan. Maybe because Paco is such a loving kid, so warm, so capable. He learns everything so quickly. And the happy ones always end up dying young; the happy and the talented, I don't know why.

The whole final phase of La Negra's pregnancy with Paco, I'll have death on the brain. At thirty years old, I, who have been thinking about death forever, will start to think about death in a way I never have before, as Paco finishes developing his lungs and digestive system in Brenda's uterus. As the due date approaches, I'm going to have the increasingly vivid impression that what's coming is a kind of death, too, and not only because her body is drawing ever closer to the edge of danger. Even if everything turns out well, Paco will no longer be inside his mother's belly, and he'll never return to it, and that is also death. He's going to experience solitude and scents, which are forms of death, and from the moment when I see him and touch him I won't be able to carry on as the same man, either. Something in me will have to die and something will also have to be born. The entire world will shed its skin when Paco is born, and I'll start to think about my own mortality, only now as someone plugged into the continuous current of species propagation. Late one night, I'm going to sit down and think about my will while Brenda is asleep, but then I'm going to realise the obvious: I have nothing to leave anyone. The car is shared, the house rented, most of the furniture was handed down and my library consists of no more than a hundred titles. Then, when I start to reflect on what I'd like to be done with my body, I'll realise that it really doesn't matter to me at all. Burial, cremation. None of it makes the slightest difference to me. It's all managed by bureaucrats in suits and ties, just like births are managed by bureaucrats in latex. But what will shock me most is the fact that this baby, who is life itself, is going to be born bearing his own death. That this unborn creature is someday going to die. That this baby will come into the world as a marked being and will have the right, the obligation, to die his own death, which is his and no one else's.

I try to explain myself, trusting that they will under-stand me: my aunt and uncle, my parents, Mauro and Mariela, Leticia – they're all mothers and fathers. Mariela looks at me, then she looks at Mauro. What happened to you two was special, I tell them. You didn't have a choice. You knew from the start that Milena would die.

'Dani, please,' whispers Dad.

Jaime goes out to the porch.

I continue: the baby was born with an expiration date, I say. What did the doctors give her? A year, maximum? That changes everything. Maybe it was even an advantage. The healthier they come out, the easier it is to forget that they're eventually going to die. You think you have all the time in the world...

Dad murmurs something so softly we can't hear it. Mum breathes deeply. When she speaks, it sounds ironic.

'Please,' she says, as though asking for more.

But Mauro says: 'It's true. With Milena it was like everything was taken to the extreme. Time was precious. Every second was worth gold.'

'It was lucky we could be there,' says Mariela, coming closer to the table. The baby will die in her arms, in the ICU, after Mariela and Mauro refuse to go through with the last operation proposed by the doctors, which would give the baby less than a three per cent chance of survival.

'What you two did was admirable,' says Mum.

'It was not admirable,' says Mariela.

'You took care of her day and night, day and night.'

'It was not admirable,' says Mariela.

'Well, for me it was!' says Mum. 'Can't I decide what I think is admirable and what isn't?'

'It's admirable if you pitied us. If you thought we were having to undergo a tragedy.'

I knew what Mariela wanted to say. When it was your turn to dance, you danced, and there was nothing grandiose or admirable in it.

'Goodness gracious…?' says Mum.

To get back to the subject at hand, I ask them all why people die. I ask them to think about it a little: why do we die? They sit there looking at me. What kills us? I ask. Having been born: that's the reason. What did we do when we decided to have a child? What did we bring them into the world for? We brought them into the world to die.

'We brought them here so they would be happy,' says Dad. 'So they can enjoy being alive. Living is worthwhile, right?'

That word: enjoy. Ale's favourite word. Enjoy, enjoy, enjoy. Life is short: let's enjoy it. Since we've been thrown into life like into the depths of a tango: let's devote ourselves to enjoyment. But enjoyment isn't guaranteed. What *is* guaranteed is death. Your child can enjoy himself or not, but when it comes to death, that's a certainty.

Mum interrupts, saying that Ale died because he thought he was king of the jungle, that nothing bad was ever going to happen to him. And maybe she's right; maybe everyone is a little bit right; any idiot can be a little bit right. I, for my part, ask her what we've got ourselves into. I say: what have we got ourselves into? Why isn't it a crime to have children? We should all have to go to jail.

'He was oblivious. He didn't think of the pain he was going to cause other people doing something like that!' says Mum, although the truth was that if he'd thought of the pain he was going to cause his mother, Alejandro wouldn't have been Alejandro. He never would have gone to Indonesia, he wouldn't have become a lifeguard, maybe he'd still be a virgin. If we thought about that, none of us would be what we are.

Dad bellows as he slams a hand down on the table. Then he starts to smooth the tablecloth with both hands, panting as if he'd just come back from a run, and apologises. Then he asks if he can show us something. He wants to show us the last thing that Alejandro wrote.

On the way back from Playa Grande, Dad is going to find a notebook in Ale's backpack. He'll start to read it in the car, from back to front. He'll tear out one page and store it in his bum-bag. It's written in red pen, in printed uppercase letters. Dad takes out the torn page, folded into eight sections, opens it and reads it aloud. Mariela and I look over his shoulder.

53

A crowd searches for the sky
And doesn't recognise its shadow
I recognise my sky
And keep close watch over my shadows
The voice passes through the barriers
That encloses this hidden thing
When I get into a condition
Leaving is my decision
And this time the barrier was dissolved
By the voice that gave the answer.

That isn't a song; no rhyme, no rhythm...

'It's the last song he wrote,' says Dad. 'He played it for me the other day over the phone. When was it, yesterday? I couldn't hear it very well. I wish I could remember the melody.'

It's not a song, I say. It's not even a poem.

'Could you let up a little, Dani?' Mariela asks me.

But I tell her: it doesn't make sense. Do you understand what he meant?

'"The voice that gave the answer"', says Dad. '"Leaving is my decision." He knew he was going to die. Don't they say that sensitive people know ahead of time?'

'I always thought his songs were a little depressing,' says Mum. 'You all thought they were nice and positive, but they were always about getting lost in nature, about finding the truth. "Let the bells ring and the universe take me." Very pretty, but it's about death.'

The son of a bitch thought he was a poet. And he wanted to die, I say. But we all want to die. Not even half a day has gone by and it already seems Ale was clairvoyant. Now apparently he knew he was going to die. Tomorrow someone's going to turn up and say Alejandro cured his blindness.

'Stop,' says Mariela, and I say: I'm going to stop, yes.

But what I want to say is that Ale was a big boy and he decided what he wanted to do and we're never going to know if he dreamed up a bolt of lightning on purpose, or if he was just an idiot, or if it was written in the stars.

'It was carelessness, he was being selfish,' says Mum.

But if there's one thing that's clear, it's that parents can't be blamed for anything, I go on. How can we be to blame, when we're the ones who get the worst of it? You're a parent and you know something like this could happen. It's not the most common thing. It's not that it's *going* to happen, necessarily, that a child dies before you; it's the least likely thing, but it can happen. You know it, and you go and have a child anyway. Maybe it's the worst thing that can happen. Maybe that's true, but it's ultimately pretty common. It's a lottery.

'It's the worst thing that can happen to you,' says Mum.

It must be different for a sibling, I say.

'Why don't you go on home?' asks Mariela.

And this is nothing. Compared with what it's going to be, it's nothing. Believe me, I tell them, we still don't feel a thing.

Mum puts a hand to her forehead.

'What do you mean we don't feel a thing?' she says.

We don't even know what we're feeling, it's all so fresh. Wait till a month or two from now, then you'll see.

'Go, take a shower, get into bed and come back tomorrow,' says Mariela. 'Alejandro's body arrives at eleven, and you know the rest.'

Marcos comes with me to the bus stop, leaving my aunt and cousin on the gravel path. They're looking off in the general direction of where Maca is sitting on a lounge chair in the back garden, at the edge of the property, half-hidden by the lemon tree.

It's four in the afternoon; there's a lot of dust in the air. Marcos is carrying the bag of Ale's clothes that I'm taking home with me. Before we sit down to wait he asks me for a smoke, and that's when he tells me that Alejandro hadn't spent the night alone in the hut. He was with his girlfriend, Ana Laura. Canary and Dwarf, from Alejandro's lifeguard team, had found her wandering on the beach. Ana Laura didn't know where she was, she didn't remember anything, except that at some point she'd been with Ale in the hut and there'd been a lot of wind. I didn't know Ale had a girlfriend. Marcos, who had only seen her in photographs, says they met a couple of weeks ago; the girl had asked him to be exclusive, and Ale had thought it was a good idea. They'd been planning to move in together in Maldonado when the season was over.

How had the girl managed to escape the lightning?

'She didn't entirely escape – she lost her memory,' says Marcos as he smokes, looking out across Giannattasio Avenue toward the lake where we'd learned to swim as kids. Then he says that Ale's board and guitar were in the hut. They'd certainly planned to spend the night there. There would be waves in the morning. He obviously wanted to get up early to surf.

'There *were* waves,' he says. 'A metre and a half easy when we got to Playa Grande today. They say the storm didn't really get started until three in the morning. Apparently Ale died at six.'

After Maca, I was the first one Marcos had talked to after he got the call from Dwarf. I was particularly drunk with pain that morning. I couldn't stop thinking about Brenda. I remember the silence that came over me when he gave me the news. It sobered me up. Suddenly, all my madness for her had been erased in one stroke. All that drama, the weight that was practically suffocating me, disappeared from one moment to the next. I remember the relief I felt.

We have time for another cigarette, and as we smoke and look out at the lake and the dust raised by the cars, I ask Marcos if he doesn't think that the most logical thing would have been for me to die instead of Ale. To my surprise Marcos replies that yes, he had always thought I was going to die young. He says he started to fear for me when I was around eighteen or nineteen. He was eight or nine and didn't really know what was going on with me, but I'd started to smoke and I seemed more and more absent and sad to him. It was during this period, Marcos says, that he stopped telling me about his day when he came home from school, because I didn't listen anymore. Or I half-listened. Sometime around then, Marcos tells me, he had a dream that I died and went to hell.

'Then you started writing, and I remember you listened to Nirvana, Nick Cave, Marilyn Manson. I was what, twelve, thirteen? Ale and I listened to them too. It was all death, death, death. Death and darkness. I imagined all of your deaths,' Marcos says then.

He says that he always imagined – because he was the youngest, he supposes – that he would be alone at the end, everyone dead but him.

I hadn't considered it an obsession until my first year of university. In my writing workshop I always got the best grades, and my professor – who in the middle of the year would personally bring my first manuscript to a publisher – would always ask me to read my work to the rest of the class. It was after one of these readings that a classmate of mine asked me, in front of everyone, what my deal with death was. Everything I wrote was full of people dying, cemeteries, blood, and so on. It caught me by surprise. I had never stopped to think about that. It was the first time a reader made me feel naked. Not that it mattered much to me at the time. I was just starting to share the things I was writing, I got good reactions, and that was enough for me.

Thinking about death had been the norm for me since 1982, when I was six years old and Grandpa Washington, my father's father, died. Starting then and for a long time, after I wondered what a person felt when they died. I wondered if it was possible to be conscious at the moment of death. If it was possible, somehow, to witness one's own death. I imagined the feeling of that instant as the truest feeling of all. I imagined it so much that I started to wish it would happen to me. I remember sitting in the sun in the back garden, in a corner where I couldn't be seen because the pine and the acacia grew together there; I remember sitting there for hours, enduring the thirst and hunger. I imagined I was dying, and at a certain point it seemed like I was, because everything turned upside down: the sounds of the birds and the cars on Giannattasio Avenue bored into me, and suddenly I could hear the beating of my heart outside my body, and the sound of my stomach surrounding me.

I never died, and I never told anyone about my fantasies. If death was ever mentioned in my family, it was as something bad. My mother, thanks to her job at the beauty salon, found out about all the deaths and illnesses in the neighbourhood and always recounted them as tragedies. She was also particularly sensitive because each one of us, her children, had had a brush with death. I had been first, with a staph infection I contracted in the hospital a few hours after I was born that kept me hospitalised for over a month, forcing my parents into a constant insomnia. Next, Alejandro had come down with peritonitis when he was six. Simultaneously, Marcos was going to catch glandular fever and Mariela, at only fourteen, was going to have a benign tumour on her hip.

When he was six or seven years old, Alejandro started in with a series of questions that he usually asked at the dinner table or in the car, whenever he got bored. He would ask, for example: 'How would you rather die: get hit by a train or have a plane fall on you?'

He wasn't eight or nine. He must have been six or seven, because it was impossible to grant any seriousness to his inquisitions; we celebrated them like strange, ingenious witticisms. Once we'd answered, Ale would come up with another pair of horrendous options, and he would keep going until someone, usually Mum, told him to be quiet. You'd be eaten by a lion, dropped into a volcano, forced to swallow a bomb. All kinds of hair-raising options. I sympathised with him to a certain extent, but I didn't like the game. I didn't like any of his options. They didn't give you time for anything, or they were so painful that the pain would surely knock you unconscious. People had strokes, their hearts burst; they choked on a piece of bread or caught a bullet or got crushed inside a car. But when I imagined dying, there was no cause of death.

Alejandro thought about death, though not every day like I did. To him, thinking about death was a necessity. Or rather, more than thinking about death per se, it was necessary to think about one's own mortality. He almost never thought about his death – how he'd like it to be, how he wouldn't like it to be. He preferred not to imagine that moment at all; he wanted to leave it open to chance. Once, when he was on one of his trips, he'd thought he was going to die. In Pichilemu, a cold, clear shoal on the Chilean coast, the lip of a five-metre wave had crashed onto him. As he was watching the son of a bitch close above him, slowly, relentlessly, he'd thought: I could die here. He says he hesitated. He'd never seen death from so close up. He was always aware of the risks he ran when he travelled in search of big waves. Here on our coast, you only got waves of that magnitude once or twice a year, and almost never in summer, so it was difficult to prepare for them. The only way to prepare for riding a big wave was by riding big waves, and Ale's trips never lasted longer than three months. In a way, on every trip he had to learn how to surf big waves all over again, and on breaks that were always new and entailed a process of familiarisation. You'd always feel the adrenaline when you went into the sea like that. You'd turn serious with fear. You wouldn't catch the first good wave that came, like you'd do in calmer waters. You'd let several sets of waves pass, you'd study them, look for the best position. The trip to Chile had been one of his solo trips, and Ale was alone on the break that afternoon. His only company, a Chilean who rented out his services as a photographer, was on the shore. As a rule, you weren't supposed to go out into rough surf alone, but Ale wasn't about to wait for anyone. He says as the wave was closing he asked himself: what am I doing here? He tried to brace for it, steeling his muscles; when the lip reached him, the force of the impact emptied his lungs with a single blow. Then it flattened him against the rock bottom and tossed him around like a rag doll until he saw colours and his lungs were on fire. He spent the rest of the afternoon and the whole night lying in his tent feeling battered, as if someone had pounded him to a pulp. After that experience, he was no longer afraid of the image of his own death. For my part, more than anything I feared the kind of illness that leaves you prostrate. Ale agreed it was one of the least desirable deaths, but it didn't terrify him and he didn't think it was his destiny.

We talked about death. We philosophised. We smoked weed and philosophised. We drank *mate* and philosophised. We drank *grapamiel*, we drank wine and talked about music, bands, we talked about his autodidactic musical process, about books, about women. When Marcos grew up, we talked about movies, video games, martial arts, we hatched thousands of projects that would unite music, film, and literature, and we philosophised. Of all our philosophical conversations, I specifically remember two: the last one, when Ale expressed his desire to be cremated, and which we held one afternoon, years ago: Ale was twenty-three and we were just breaking in the lair, and I was thirty. Brenda was pregnant with Paco, and I was obsessed with the idea that we had lost something fundamental on leaving the births and burials of our people in the hands of doctors and bureaucrats. Power. That was the only word I had to name what we'd lost. Power over our own lives.

That afternoon will be one of the first ones we spend with the lair fully finished, and Ale and I are going to eat outside with Marcos (nineteen) and my father (sixty) around a green plastic table on the still-unsettled earth. Three metres away, my father's garden will look scrawny and dejected, having suffered the effects of dust and noise during the months of construction. When a family member died, why were we unable to personally take care of the body? My hypothesis was that if you buried your own dead, it would help you mourn. I thought that a process that normally took years could be shortened to hours. And who knew if it wasn't the same for the dead person? Even if he was already dead, who could say for sure it didn't affect him somehow that the last hands to touch him were hands that knew and loved him?

'That's only if you believe in the spirit,' I remember Alejandro objecting.

'But all funeral rites are based on the belief in the spirit. They help propel the dead person's spirit on their journey to the other world.' That was Marcos, who had been in the habit of reading *The Iliad* once a year since he was twelve.

'For me, the body and soul are a single thing, and there's no other world to go to,' Ale will say then. He wasn't interested in that part. As long as the thing worked for the people left behind, that was enough for him.

The other conversation I remember happened after Milena was buried. So that the baby wouldn't lie there alone, Mum had had the idea to buy a cemetery plot where the whole family could fit. There was nothing intrinsically wrong with her decision, except for the fact that she'd taken it without consulting us. Our response wasn't what she expected. Ale, who would soon follow Milena, was the first to refuse to be buried. He was reaching the end of his experiment living with Lucía in her apartment in Montevideo; he was frustrated, and his reply was dry and unequivocal.

'Please do me the favour of burning me up. Toss my ashes in the ocean, done and done.'

Marcos preferred fire too. I wasn't even remotely tempted by the idea of rotting alongside my family, but I was a little more restrained and said I wasn't sure, I'd have to think about it.

Alejandro will leave the lair for good in April, ten months before he vanishes, when he moves with Lucía, after they've been living behind my parents' house for over a year. He doesn't love her anymore, he would never have a baby with her – it's with her that he realises he wasn't meant to have kids – but he'll move with her anyway. Her grandmother is going to buy an apartment in Montevideo on 18 de Julio Avenue. It's the last place that Ale, who has spent years dreaming of a plot of land in the east, would want to go. But it's close to the Fine Arts Institute, where he has registered to study composition at the Music School and where he's a member of the chorus, and he figures it's the perfect opportunity to get out of Mum and Dad's house once and for all and take a step toward maturity. He'll move with the hope that, just as I've been telling him, his relationship with Lucía will have a better chance of rekindling, or will at least take a clearer path, if they're living on their own and free of external influences.

'If this move doesn't work out, I always have Rocha at the end of the year,' he'll tell me on one of his last nights in the lair. 'I can start the pre-season in November, or October. In September if I need to. But I'm definitely not going back to the lair. That phase is over.'

He will take a conscious step in the wrong direction, going west instead of east, to the city instead of the beach, saying that things with Lucía will get better, knowing it's not going to happen. In a master stroke, Alejandro will buy all the necessary materials to build a recording studio in the last of the new apartment's five bedrooms. He will be the one, moreover, who takes care of cleaning the apartment, repairing part of the dining room floor, painting the kitchen and even packing up Lucía's clothes. Meanwhile, she grows more and more absent as the move approaches, consumed by work and medical needs. Lucía won't do anything for the move except put up obstacles.

'It's like she isn't moving at all,' Alejandro will say.

The last obstacle will involve the choice of moving van. Alejandro will talk to the vegetable vendor on the corner, who will offer his truck; all of their things will fit perfectly well, and it would be washed and disinfected. Lucía will die of disgust at the idea of putting her things in a vegetable truck – it will all end up smelling like a market stall – and she'll decide to hire a separate truck for herself, a moving van that charges triple what the vegetable vendor does.

'So we're moving in separate trucks,' Ale will say.

You're moving together, but separately.

'Together-apart,' he'll say. 'That's what this chapter of our relationship is called.'

The day of the move, I tell him, just help her unload her things, leave yours in the vegetable truck, give the guy some extra cash and have him take you to Rocha.

'To hell with Rocha,' he'll say. 'Straight to Costa Rica. I'll take a taxi to Costa Rica.'

We'll be drinking *grapamiel*, smoking weed with the sliding window open, when we hear the sound of leaves outside, the patter of feet over a carpet of dry leaves. It's going to be a weasel but still, lit by the moon, rolling with laughter, we look out into the garden in case Lucía is hiding behind a tree or in the bushes.

Twenty-four hours before the move, Lucía will admit that the truck she hired is too big, her things won't even take up a fifth of the space, and she proposes that Ale put his things in with hers. Lucía pays for the van, to make up a little for how absent she's been lately. They move together-together, then, but the next day, after inaugural sex in the apartment, Lucía will lose her set of keys. They'll search the house high and low. Next they'll go out into the street, and then investigate fruitlessly in several of the shops on the block. That night Lucía won't sleep a wink, imagining that the maniac who found her keys is going to break in as soon as she falls asleep. She's a voluptuous, beautiful girl; a large and radiant pony. She takes up a lot of space. She can fill an entire house with her voice, just like Alejandro. Their conversations can be heard from a distance. Lucía isn't about to spend another sleepless night, so Alejandro is tasked with changing the locks that same day while she's at work. Ale is going to end up spending exactly the amount he saved on the truck. It won't even occur to her to pay half.

'I'm thinking that the pre-season will start early this year, just as predicted,' Alejandro will tell me the first time I go round to see the apartment and help him with the furniture. Lucía is gone the whole day, just as she was before the move. When she comes back she's too exhausted or nervous or it's too late to lift a finger, and Ale is the one who will take care of organising everything, in addition to the shopping and cooking.

That particular afternoon, Lucía will burst through the door at sunset and she won't be able to hide her disappointment at finding us drinking beer in her armchairs, listening to music, the living room emptied of boxes except for the ones filled with books, neatly lined up beneath the shelves. She'll run straight to the bathroom saying she'll be right back. After a minute, Ale will go see what's wrong. Five minutes later I'm still alone in the living room with a beer and a joint, I'm going to start leafing through the books in the boxes.

'Maybe you should go,' Ale will tell me from the alcove that leads to the hallway.

'No! He shouldn't leave!' Lucía will yell from the bathroom. 'I'll be right out!'

We'll end up unpacking all the books. There will be a lot of space left on the shelves, which will be filled with photos and knickknacks. Lucía emerges when we're halfway finished, her cheeks shining. Without mentioning what happened, she's going to take a sip from Alejandro's glass and start rearranging the books we already organised. Then she's going to explain to us that she wants to separate her books from the ones her uncle gave her. She'll start talking about her uncle and her father, and how ever since her father's death her uncle has started to treat her just like her father used to do. He'll stop giving her horrible nicknames; he'll call her Lucecita like her father did, and in the very same tone of voice, the same little lilt on the last syllable. Just as her father did, her uncle will call her three times a week and ask her about the same things: work, whether she's eating well, her love life, whether she needs cash. Like her father, every once in a while he'll give her an unexpected gift. Could be anything: an appliance, a set of crystal glasses, a pair of trainers, a piece of furniture he doesn't use anymore. So every time she talks to her uncle, Lucía will think of her father. She's going to have the impression that her father is watching over her through her uncle. At first, she'll think it's a strategy of her uncle's so she won't feel completely abandoned, then she'll speculate that maybe her father had left instructions to his little brother about how to take care of her. That will comfort her, but not for long. At a certain point it will start to seem violent and sinister and Lucía will start to experience her loss as double: her father's death has taken her father from her and also her uncle, and when Lucía talks to her uncle she is talking to a dead man who constantly reminds her of another dead man. I'm going to end up taking some of the uncle's books home with me.

'You can take any of his books except the one about Frida Kahlo – I'm interested in that one,' Lucía will say, more composed now, almost in confidence, when she finishes placing them on the highest shelf. I'm going to choose the first volume of Borges' *Complete Works*, published by Emecé, and two or three others.

From the very first day in the new apartment, while he unpacks and organises, Alejandro is going to take a couple of hours a day to work on the recording studio. Contrary to what he'd imagined, it doesn't seem to bring much reassurance to Lucía, who doesn't see it as a guarantee of the relationship's longevity. I'm not going to witness the process, because I won't want to set foot in the apartment for a while, but he tells me about it over the phone.

With his own two hands, Ale cuts the pine boards and the plywood sheets. He has the plaster panels sent off to be cut. He covers them with carpet, and joins the plywood to the carpeted panels, attaching them to the pine boards after filling the spaces with foam. He goes back and forth to the hardware store. After a month, when it's all ready, I'll go and see how it's turned out. Inside the back bedroom I'm going to find a three-by-three-metre cabin built against one of the inner walls, leaving enough room to walk around and for the djembe, the lute and the electric and bass guitars, all arranged neatly in a corner. The cabin will be ultra-silent, hermetic, and it will look professional. It won't have any ventilation, but it will have an acrylic plate that acts as a window to let in light. Between the drum kit and the computer there will be room for a chair. It will be very hot in there. Alejandro will have dedicated a lot of time and effort to the space, all the while knowing that one day, not too far in the future, he'll have to take it apart. He's going to say so himself the third and last time I visit him there. We'll be drinking wine and eating salami, cheese and bread, the same thing he eats every day, sitting in the kitchen with its two refrigerators – one for him and another for Lucía, who is in treatment for some digestive problem and can't eat meat or flour.

'I'm recording an album. I'm going to make the most of the studio. And when I finish it I'll get the fuck out of here.' Alejandro's words.

His time in the apartment, then, is going to be measured by how long he takes to record his album, into which he'll incorporate everything he is learning at the Music School and in the Bellas Artes choir, where they teach him to sing with his whole face. That will have an immediate effect on his voice; it becomes more relaxed, more confident than ever. I won't visit him at all during that final period, which lasts two months, through September. I don't want to run the risk of seeing Lucía again. I don't want to be part of the sad memories filling up her apartment. I'm going to hear several of the new songs when I meet up with Ale at my parents' house and when he comes to my place one Sunday for a barbecue, the first he's had since he moved. I'll hear him complain that he can barely go outside. The racket of Montevideo makes him dizzy, the smells, all the excitement you have to breathe in, all the gazes so full of intentions, so he spends practically all day in the studio. He's afraid the album is growing too baroque; he's getting the hang of the recording programme, and he's really piling it on.

'I'd spend a year on it if I could, but I don't know how much longer I can stick it out. I'm going to have to simplify.'

I'll wonder if he hasn't built the studio precisely in order to complicate his escape. I'm going to imagine him obsessing over the album project until summer starts, then returning to the apartment after the season in

Rocha to go on recording an album that's been endlessly fine-tuned, Ale playing all the instruments, singing all the voices, controlling everything, surrounded by the most hostile environment possible, more focused than ever for that very reason.

The afternoon of the barbecue, drunk and high, I'm going to tell Alejandro my fantasy. Together, we're going to imagine that he ends up staying forever in the apartment on 18 de Julio, spending nearly the entire day in his hermetic three-by-three trap. So engrossed will he be in his music that he and Lucía don't even talk anymore, and they end up living the way they were going to move in the first place, together but apart. They don't sleep together anymore; Lucía even finds herself a new boyfriend, and the two of them tolerate Alejandro's presence in the apartment, because by that point he's almost a ghost. If he comes out of the studio, it's only to go to the bathroom or make something to eat. At a certain point, we come up with the idea that one night the phone rings and it's the first-floor neighbours, an old couple: they have a broken pipe, their house is flooded, they need help. In our fantasy Lucía doesn't even want to hear about Alejandro going down to give them a hand, but Ale goes and solves their problem, and then the old couple grows fond of him and they start to call him to fix things for them. One day another neighbour calls him after one whole side of his apartment loses electricity; he got Ale's number from the first-floor neighbours, who had wonderful things to say about him, and Ale ends up practically becoming a maintenance man for the whole building. They call him from every floor, they invite him to eat, to have a drink, he ends up sleeping with a teenage girl living on the third floor. No, he doesn't sleep with anyone: except for Ale and Lucía, it's all old people living in the building. There's one old lady who seems incapable of taking her high heels off, even to sleep; Ale goes up to play guitar for her. Lucía can't take it anymore and she throws him out. The old couple from the first floor stop him when he passes by their door carrying his suitcases. They won't let him go; they call in the other the old folks from the building, and in their meeting they decide to fix up an abandoned room in the basement. Ale lives there for decades on a salary that's enough for him to eat his fill, and he even reaches an agreement with Lucía: she lets him use the studio when she's out, which is over ten hours a day.

But the reality is that Alejandro will finish recording the album around mid-spring, and when he does he'll leave Lucía's house and live in mine in Parque del Plata until November, when he heads to Rocha. The walls of the studio, which take him and a friend three hours to dismantle, will be left in my storage room, along with the foam pieces and the extra rolls of carpet. He will save the materials with the idea of maybe setting up another studio in the little house he'll buy or build not long from now, probably in Santa Ana or Cuchilla Alta.

When I arrive home on the fateful afternoon of 9th February, after dropping the bag of Ale's clothes on the kitchen floor, I go straight to the storage room and start to take everything out. I pull out the studio walls. I take out the door, which is the heaviest part. I take out the rolls of carpet and the foam. The idea is to drag everything to the street so the dustcart or someone else could take it away, but all the day's exhaustion soon comes over me, along with an unbearable pain in my neck and arms, and I leave it all scattered on the grass.

At 11.15 pm I get a call from an unknown number. I remember wishing for it to be something that had nothing to do with Ale. Anything else: a work problem, even a survey. But it was Agustina, Ale's first girlfriend.

I had been present the day Alejandro declared his love to her. Ale was taking an English class at the Anglo-Uruguay Institute in Lagomar, where I worked. Agustina, who was beautiful, with shy blue eyes, was also preparing for an advanced exam, the Cambridge Advance Certificate in English, and she was my student. Our classes ended at the same time. Ale and I would take the bus to Shangrilá, and Agustina would catch her bus to El Pinar on the other side of the street. That afternoon, Ale did get on the bus and pay for his ticket, but then he got off at the next stop. 'It's now or never,' he told me. 'I'm going to tell Agustina how I feel.'

I watched him run across the street. From then on, they were nearly inseparable. They saw each other during the day and she'd call him at night, sometimes in the early morning. Agustina said that her stepfather harassed her, and she'd call Alejandro two or three nights a week to tell him she was in the street, asking him to come meet her. The phone would ring and wake my parents, and they'd try to dissuade him any way they could from going out to find her.

'What is that girl doing to you? Don't let her manipulate you,' my mother told him.

But Ale was in love, he was getting laid for the first time, and he'd go out at night and run along the side of the road so he wouldn't die of cold waiting at the bus stop. Sometimes he'd run five kilometres without a bus going by. When one finally appeared, he'd get on. And he'd keep her company. They'd walk through the streets of El Pinar. They'd go as far as the beach. If they could, they'd go back to her house to sleep in her little bed. Ale suffered for her. Several times he talked about going to confront the stepfather, but whenever he did run into him, the stepfather was friendly to him, as if nothing out of the ordinary were going on.

At first, when she tells me her name, I don't know which Agustina she could be. Then, with her last name, Figueroa, the memory returns. They had reconnected, she and Ale, over the years. They were always explosive encounters, and they both always ended up reluctantly admitting that they weren't meant for each other. She needed to talk to me. She'd got my number from Marcos, with whom she had a friend in common. Not fifteen minutes ago, Alejandro had appeared to her in her bedroom. She was asleep and something had woken her: Alejandro was standing next to her bed, beautiful, smiling the sweetest smile. One of his arms was glowing.

'I can't stop shaking while I'm telling you this,' Agustina said.

Although Alejandro's ghost didn't speak, Agustina had understood that he was waiting for her permission to get in bed with her. But Agustina was so afraid that she'd started to cry, which had made him disappear. That was when she'd opened Facebook and visited Ale's page, and only then had she found out.

She cries for a while on the other end of the line. Then, through her tears, she talks about how important I'd been for them. They had discovered rock music through me. Ale had made her cassettes with my albums: Dirty Three, Violent Femmes, the Stone Temple Pilots.

'You remember the box set of Smashing Pumpkins B-sides?'

Then she asks me if I've seen Alejandro's Facebook page. Her voice breaks with indignation. People were filling his wall with photos and videos and with messages directed to him, as if Ale were going to receive them via internet. His account was turning into a souvenir album. Worse, into a gravestone. We should meet for coffee one of these days, she says. She didn't know if she'd be able to gather the courage to go to the wake, but one day we'd have to get together and talk. She was going to need it.

'I can tell you a thousand stories about Ale that no one knows,' she says, although I wasn't writing about him yet. It hadn't even occurred to me.

The conversation with Agustina sends me out into the street. It had been a long time since we'd had two dry nights in a row. Instead of walking on side streets as I usually do, I go along the Interbalnearia. By my house, the Interbalnearia stretches out in a perfect straight line that extends for five kilometres, until it takes a sudden curve at the Solís Chico Creek. I think about going to Clara's house. I want to sleep in someone's arms, but I shudder when I remember Agustina's story, Ale's ghost trying to get in her bed, and I don't want to turn off the lights. I walk as far as the traffic light and turn around.

To my surprise, I sleep soundly again. This time I have a dream that's almost impossible to wake from. I was lying down on a stretch of grass, looking up at the sky, and everything was calm until I noticed something plummeting toward me from above. It was falling straight toward my chest. I only realised it was Ale when it was about to crash into me. Then it stopped short; the speed of the shaggy thing slowed to zero, and it started floating around my body. It was wrapped in its own hair and I could barely distinguish parts of Alejandro's face inside the tangle. Meanwhile, it sniffed me like a puppy looking for its mother's teat. And it wouldn't stop, no matter how much I repeated to it, over and over: there's no body for you here, there's no body here.

The morning of the wake, after I write down my dream, I sit thinking about how it could be possible for Brenda to vanish from my mind from one second to the next. Her image no longer keeps me awake at night, and if I think about her at all, she appears as something distant, harmless. After my shower I put on Ale's Adidas and I get to my parents' house a little before eleven. Mariela, Uncle Jaime and Aunt Laura are all there. Dad is still getting dressed to go and receive the body. He's sitting on a dining room chair and putting on his shoes. Mum is watching him.

Mumsy, Veteran, I greet them, realising a second later, from their startled faces, that I've used Alejandro's names for them.

The TV is on but muted. When she sees me looking at the screen, Mum tells me they haven't said anything about Ale on the morning news. One single day, that's how long his story had lasted on TV. Then she wants to know if Mariela and I are going to go with them now to Salhón, or if we'd come later. It seems to me that Mum and Dad wanted to be alone for a while with Alejandro's body. Mariela has the same impression; I can tell when our eyes meet. I sense that they don't want Jaime and Laura's company either during these first moments, but my aunt and uncle don't take the hint. Aunt Laura, in fact, has attached herself to my mother's arm. I hear her say she hadn't been able to sleep all night: she couldn't stop thinking about Ale, about the moment he passed, the fear he must have felt there in the hut, poor thing.

'I heard thunder during the night, but I went out to the balcony and there was no thunder,' says Laura.

Mum had heard it too. She hadn't been able to sleep either.

'I don't know how I'm going to manage to sleep on stormy nights,' she says.

That's when I ask Mariela about Marcos, who is in the back garden.

'What was my little boy thinking about?' Mum is saying. 'I close my eyes and I see him calling to me, with lightning all around him.'

'Sole, Soledad,' my aunt consoles her. 'I'm sure he thought about you in his last moments. You're his mother.'

Mariela and I are going out through the sliding door when my mother's voice stops us to let us know that Marcos has broken up with Macarena. He'd kicked her out last night.

'At ten o'clock we heard knocking on the door and it was Maca, carrying her suitcases, coming to say goodbye. Her parents were on their way to pick her up. She was devastated. I don't know how Marcos could do it. Do you all want to kill us with sadness?'

Marcos is playing guitar in the sun in the doorway to the lair. He's wearing sunglasses, and instead of his usual ponytail, he's left his hair down.

'I should have done it sooner,' he cuts us off. 'It was already done. It had to be yesterday, no matter what. How many things have I been depriving myself of over all these years? I deprived myself of going to Chile with Ale. He invited me to Recife and Indonesia and I always said no, I can't. And all because of money and our plans as a couple. And now Alejandro is dead. How long should I have waited to break up with her? Would it have been better after he was buried? How long? A week? A month? We're alive today, who knows about tomorrow.'

Maca seemed like she was made for Marcos. They were both energetic, both planners, they were the same age, one danced, the other made films, both had a special taste for LSD. I remembered the night when I'd tripped with them and Ale in the lair, not long before Ale headed off for his last season at Rocha. We took half a tab each,

75

and at one point we were listening to songs on YouTube and the songs were changing too fast. There'd been too much chatter for my taste. They commented too much on what was happening. If it wasn't a remark about the music, they'd start comparing perceptions or thinking back to other acid-fuelled nights. There was a moment when Maca had a fit of laughter and wanted to bring all of us into her trip. Marcos, a little forced, had gone along. The tension eating away at them was already there and it made me feel bad, but I stayed a while longer. I don't remember who put on *The Dark Side of the Moon*; we spent a good while listening to it and contemplating the cover of the album on the computer screen. The coloured beams of light emanating from the pyramid shifted and were cast off the screen, placid, into the lair. It was a beautiful and simple sight, but even that was received with exaggerated fanfare, and not long after that I left to go to bed, feeling like a bitter old man.

At thirteen, Mariela will have already finished piano classes at the conservatory. In a white plastic chair, on the guitar she takes from Marcos's hands, she starts to strum 'Come As You Are', the acoustic Nirvana song she'll teach Ale when Ale wants to learn guitar at age fourteen. She doesn't make it halfway through the song before she has to stop. Then Marcos takes the guitar inside. Before coming out again, he opens his computer and puts on the album Alejandro would record in his infamous portable studio in Lucía's apartment. I can't stop thinking about how Ale's death is like a bomb, and Maca its first victim. Images from some film come into my mind: people being hit by the expansive waves of the nuclear blast. The wave catches up to them as they run, fleeing the explosion, and a nuclear wind X-rays them for an instant. Their black skeletons show through their skin, and then they fall to dust.

I'm imagining this when Marcos notices I'm wearing Alejandro's Adidas, and he asks me if they're tight. Just a little, I answer. The uncomfortable thing is his footprint, which doesn't fit the shape of my foot. Mariela, looking at my trainers, asks if she can give me some advice, and then she advises me not to wear them.

'You shouldn't wear dead people's shoes,' she says. I asked her why not, and if she replies, I don't hear her; I'm distracted by the beginning of 'Wherever You Go'. It's the tune I've been humming since early that morning. I'd hummed it on the bus. I'd got up with that tune in my head, though I hadn't realised what it was.

The song dates from the time just before Alejandro moved to Montevideo. The chorus says: 'Wherever you go, your home is inside.' Though we'd never talked about it, I'd always thought that with this song Ale had been trying to respond, not at all subtly, to my persistent instigation that he leave the lair once and for all, a lair I had vehemently opposed from the get-go, ever since Ale told me about his plan to build something for himself behind Mum and Dad's house so he could have more independence. He was twenty-three then.

Wouldn't he rather have total independence? Didn't he realise that he was going to go on living in the same mental space as his parents did? Didn't he realise that was what they wanted? That if they had their wish we would all live on the same block?

I was thirty, about to have my first child, and I'd been out of the house for seven years; I only wished I'd left sooner. I had long since become an expert on Mum and Dad. In a way, they were the ones who had given me a writer's eye. I described their modus operandi to Alejandro, I listed their weaknesses and strengths, but Ale didn't see what I did. Some of my reasonings seemed obvious to him, but they didn't affect him like they did me. Or perhaps he had also got ahead of me there, in forgiving our parents. Or, plainly and simply, freedom for him meant something different. He was still young, he wanted to travel, and I let him be. We only returned to the subject seven years later, when his relationship with Lucía was hitting a critical point, when the two of them were living in the lair and the possibility of moving to the apartment on 18 de Julio suddenly arose. How could he have a real relationship with a woman if he was living at his parents' house? They'd always be like two children as long as they were there.

And move for your music, I told him: all the music you've written until now, you wrote here. The first destination of every song you compose is Mum and Dad's ears. You jump up to show them. And if not them, you come and play it for one of us if we're around. And what are we going to tell you? How nice, Alejandrito, your songs are so pretty? Do we have to like them all? What are you, eight years old? What music would you make if you were on your own? A person has to grow. You have to discover your own mind.

Will he not want to leave his childhood home because he knows he's going to die young? Will he want to be with his family as much as possible before his time comes, or is it that it's harder for him than for the rest of us? Even Marcos, four years younger than Ale, will leave home before him. Yes, he'll go to live with an aunt of Maca's in less than ideal conditions, and later, beset by problems of money and space, he'll find himself forced to come back and live in the place Alejandro left empty. Will this be the reason – because he never fully leaves the womb – why Alejandro's songs will avoid pain, always talking instead about a nebulous melding with nature?

When the song is over, I tell Marcos and Mariela my dream about Ale plummeting from the sky. He was a hairy thing, like Cousin Itt on The Addams Family, and he sniffed me all over like a puppy. Then I ask them if they had dreamt. Mariela hadn't. Marcos thinks he did, but he can't remember what he'd dreamt about.

Maybe I shouldn't say this, I remember saying then, but I can't imagine Alejandro dying any other way. I swear I can't picture him dying under a car or lying in a hospital bed. Can you all?

Mariela shakes her head, her eyes closed, following the rhythm of the music.

'I can't talk right now,' she says.

Ale's death fit with his personality, don't you think? Riding a wave, the way he almost died in Pichilemu, was the only other way I could imagine him going.

'Ale would have preferred a wave,' said Marcos. 'He would have preferred to die on a break. Puerto Escondido, Grajagan, Uluwatu.'

If he'd been hit by a car, that might have been reason to get angry. If he'd been hit by a car, maybe I would have even gone to find the fucker who was driving and kicked his arse. But as things were, who could you get mad at? That's why it broke my heart to see Mum cursing the storm. How can you get mad at a storm? As if the storm were some son of a bitch who had wanted to kill him on purpose. You're not in touch with reality if you think that way. What world do you live in? Injustice, injustice!

'No, there's no injustice,' said Marcos.

I didn't know of anyone who'd had such a coherent death. Pablo Vázquez, who went to school with me, sixteen years old, had copped it in a car crash; the guy driving was drunk. What kind of consolation could you find in that? My friend Sandra, who Marcos and Mariela never met, had a four-year-old son, Miguel: he copped it in a car crash, too. His father was driving, and the father survived without a scratch. Felipe Garmona,

Marcos's friend, overdosed on coke. Juan Andrés had shot himself because a girl dumped him. Jorgito Viana had hung himself in the middle of a field after taking mushrooms three days in a row. I told them about the case of a kid who'd studied at the Anglo Institute. I couldn't remember his name, he hadn't been my student; he had a Basque surname. His case had been famous – they'd shown it on TV, like Ale's. He'd been run over during the La Pedrera carnival. Eighteen years old. The kid decided to cut the night short and go back alone to the house he was renting with a group of friends. He was going along nice and calm, walking down the street, and a car that was coming toward him on the other side of the street ran him down: the driver's girlfriend was giving him a blow job, and the guy had lost control of the wheel. Now that was grotesque. Now there you can get angry, no problem. I can understand it then. But Playa Grande was a paradisiacal bay. It looked like Brazil, with those hills running right into the sea, the pine woods behind them. Alejandro himself used to call it paradise, right? That's why he chose to spend a third of the year there, in the place where he's going to die almost by statistical proba-bility. Where he's going to be electrocuted by a bolt of lightning that can generate five times more heat than the surface of the sun. And he's going to die with the girl, board and guitar beside him – his favourite things. What if you got the death you deserved? What if death was the moment when a person's character was finally revealed? Who were those people who managed to die such trans-parent deaths? What did the son of a bitch leave for *us*? How were we going to have to die, if we wanted to live up to his death?

'Have we gone crazy or were we crazy already?' asks Mariela.

A few minutes later – as we're getting ready to go

to the viewing room where Mum and Dad have already spent too long alone with the body – it occurs to Marcos, in a fit of lucidity, to bring the computer with Alejandro's music.

The funeral home is behind the monstrosity that is the Costa Urbana Shopping Centre, on the other side of the street that encircles it. The sun is shining, and people are sitting on the stairs up to the entrance of the Civic Centre, where all the public offices are. Mariela walks ahead of us. She goes in through the brown glass-paned door carrying the computer and the speakers, and instead of going straight to see Alejandro, she finds a power socket beside a little table, moves a decorative flower vase to the floor, and spends some time connecting the devices and looking for the file with Alejandro's music. Marcos, who has already viewed the body, goes straight to Mum and Dad, who are standing in the doorway of the room with the coffin, flanked by my aunt and uncle, as if waiting to receive the first mourners. He gives each of them a long hug.

The coffin, dark brown and shining, is closed except for the upper lid, showing Alejandro's shrouded face. It's the only skin you can see, the skin of his face, and it's pale. Several long curls have escaped the cloth, blond and white and brown. His half-open mouth reveals his front teeth, and there's something strange on his lip, though I can't figure out what it is.

'There's Alejandrito,' murmurs Mum, standing to my right. 'There's your brother.'

But if that were Alejandro, he would say something. I look at his teeth. They're his teeth, the front two ones shaped like the prow of a ship, but it isn't him.

'That's where he bit himself,' says Marcos, who has come to stand to my left, and he touches Ale's lower lip. It was now the lower lip of no one. That was what had seemed strange, the too-smooth spot that Marcos is lightly touching as I stroke Ale's curls and think: my children should be here to see and touch their dead uncle. What did Paco and Juan know about death? They had seen the occasional dead dog beside the road, some birds, frogs, fish, but nothing more. Juan had gone crazy one afternoon on the beach when he saw a fisherman reel in a sea bass and leave it on the sand to die. He yelled at the poor guy to throw the fish back into the water, and he yelled at us, at Brenda and me, to back him up, while the bass flopped around out of its element. The tears started flowing, and he was so agitated we had to take him home. I was remembering the expression on the fisherman's face as he scrutinised me, as though asking me what kind of child I was raising, when Mum leaned over the coffin, opened one of Ale's eyelids, said 'my baby' to his indifferent pupil and started to cry over him.

Ale's music is playing, and Marcos and I go into the other room. Mariela, as if she's been waiting her turn, goes into the room with the coffin. The music muffles the sobs and wails, though it doesn't drown them out entirely, and Marcos and I sit for a good half hour on the sofa against the wall opposite the computer. At one point four guys in suits file by, each carrying a floral arrangement. They bring them to Alejandro's room before re-emerging in single file. Then Marcos says we're going to have to do something with Ale's music. One of these days we're going to have to get together and make a selection of songs and bring it to a label.

'Just listen to this music,' he says. 'This music needs to be out in the world.'

Marcos had been Alejandro's first fan. He and his

group of friends from kung fu practically idolised him. They had shared countless nights of drunkenness, of playing loudly, of musical connection. Marcos's friends invited Ale to play at their parties, and it was with one of them, Sebita, that he ultimately formed Voice Over, a furious duo of guitar and drums with which Ale would record his first homemade albums. They will break up after a couple of years – Sebita didn't put in the effort, while Ale started taking lessons with Topo, from the band Buenos Muchachos – and from then on, he'll play solo. He'll learn to play drums and to use the software that means he won't need anyone else. He'll have a few ephemeral groups again, all with amateur musicians, but mostly he'll be a one-man band. I'll offer several times to take his albums to labels like Bizarro or Ayuí, but he'll refuse. I'm never sure if he really doesn't feel the need for his music to go public, or if he's just scared of rejection, but I understand that feeling of wanting to remain pure, unknown. Ale believed in the act of making music. In the experience of the moment of playing. That experience was the primary thing; really, it was the only thing. Much of his training happened during the time when I'd moved away from literature, after my third book. I decided I would only write again if I were able to recover my original innocence, and Ale and I had many a discussion about purity. How long would his voice and his music, playing now over the speakers, survive him? Was he great? On this particular afternoon, what does it matter?

When the first round of mourners finally arrives, we stand to be hugged and then sit back down. We carry on like this for a good while. Before we abandon our spot, Marcos rests his head on my shoulder and starts to sing in a low voice, accompanying Ale's. Overcome with emotion, it's not long before he loses all sense of shame and starts to sing louder, unafraid of being heard. I would have done the same, but I'm distracted by the startling certainty that some people here don't know that the songs playing over the speakers had been composed by the deceased. People like the employees of Mum's hair salon – today dressed in civilian clothes, no caps or aprons – squeezed in together on the sofa across from us. They're unable to hide their horror at seeing us this way, leaning against each other and singing along to the chorus like a couple of drunks.

Except for once when I go back into the main building, I spend the next hour or so on a sunny bench in the plaza, smoking and welcoming and watching the hordes of people who overflow the rooms and invade the patio – over two hundred of them. Alejandro's classmates from his PE course are here, and lifeguards from the area, friends from the neighbourhood, drinking buddies and old classmates. It shouldn't have surprised me that most of them knew who I was even though I'd never seen them in my life; not even when they tell me their names can I place them right away. Some of them come over and greet me without introducing themselves, and their effusiveness tells me that at some point, somewhere, we had met. Agustina isn't here.

Natalia and Rafael, whom I know through stories and photos, are the last ones I greet. They will live with my brother for three months in Indonesia, where they'll ask him to be best man at their wedding in an open-air temple. Indonesia, where Rafa will purge all the sorrow and resentment built up in his heart, dreaming about and talking every night to his father, who committed suicide; where Alejandro will also have the most intense dreams of his life, chalking it up to the Mefloquine and the atmosphere impregnated with Hinduism. Squeezing my shoulders in his big hands, looking me in the eyes, Rafa tells me that Ale always said I was the most spiritual of our siblings. Beside him, Natalia, incredibly beautiful with a white ribbon in her hair, nods with raised eyebrows. They give the impression of confessing something extremely important, and I'm overcome by a fit of laughter. Suddenly all three of us are cracking up.

'He always said it,' laughs Natalia. 'He said: Dani is the most spiritual of us all…'

You must have heard wrong, I tell them. He must have said I had the biggest head.

'Ale told us…' laughs Rafael.

He must have said I was the most negative.

'Spiritual,' Natalia gasps. 'He said spiritual.'

Now, you know a person has to be really spiritual before they can realise who the most spiritual one is, I tell them.

'Yes, yes, yes, yes, it's true, it's true…' they both laugh.

We have the good sense to say goodbye with a hug before the laughter is extinguished, and I make my way through the crowd without meeting anyone's eyes. Inside, it's cool and Ale's music is playing more softly now; I only hear it as I walk past the speakers. It fades away when I enter the room with the coffin, where I see Grandma Amor sitting down, flanked by my mother and Aunt Laura. Mum and Laura are leaning forward a little and talking to each other, but Grandma isn't participating in the crossfire; she's just looking at the coffin and the air above it and she barely notices me when I bend down to give her a hug and a kiss.

I hadn't seen her arrive. Her name is Soledad, like my mum's, but she will be Grandma Amor or just Amor starting when her first grandchild, Viviana, gives her the nickname.

'Did you see? What a lovely feather,' Grandma tells me, pointing to the coffin.

What feather, Grandma?

'A young boy came and put it there, a black boy.'

On the coffin, at the height of Ale's chest, lies a black feather longer than my hand. It's beautiful, lush but compact; it looks like it's been styled.

'It was beautiful' says Grandma. 'He came in, put the feather on the coffin, and left.'

'Yes, he's gone,' adds Mum, visibly moved. 'He was thin, very young. He was wearing red shorts, and I really couldn't say who he was.'

There is no boy in shorts inside or on the patio, and there are only two or three black people at the wake. One of them is El Negro Laguna, a childhood friend of mine who lives on the lake where we learned to swim. The Tarzan rope had been his; it hung from a eucalyptus behind his house, over the shore.

The boy isn't on the street, either. He isn't on the stairs in front of the Civic Centre and he isn't in the plaza, which I reach by skirting the shopping centre through the parking lot access, and where I stop to smoke on the other side of the railing while studying each of the groups of kids camped out in the shade of the wall.

I think twice before answering Brenda's call. She says she's just calling to send me a big hug during this difficult moment. I tell her she can come to the wake if she wants, that maybe it's not such a bad idea for the boys to see Ale. This wasn't the usual, miserable kind of funeral.

'Kids have their own process,' she says. 'I don't know if it's necessary for them to see so much grown-up sadness. It's different for them. Right now they're playing in the pool...'

I don't let her finish. There are around two or maybe three hundred people. I say: don't ask me how Alejandro managed to have so many friends. And: strange things are happening. The sadness she was talking about isn't in the air. A lot of people had come. I don't even know most of them, but I know their stories with Ale because Ale told them to me. Alejandro talked about all his friends to the rest of his friends and he talked to all of them about us and everyone knew about everyone else, I say. And he spoke well about people, he never said bad things. I say: I hardly ever heard him talk badly about one of his friends, and if he did he always sounded really sad about having to do it. And: since Ale was a happy guy, there's happiness, I swear. His friends are happy to see him, you know? Alejandro visited them, his friends came to see him. Can you hear me?

'You're cutting out a little,' she says.

You could sense all of that. And now a feather had appeared on top of the coffin and we didn't know who had put it there. A black kid, supposedly, but he was nowhere to be found. I don't know where Alejandro could have met a kid like that, one who would bring him a feather. He sounds like a street kid, I said. You can't imagine the feather. Black, big, I don't know what type of bird it could be from, but it was just what we needed. I mean, before, without the feather, the coffin was one thing. You can't hear me at all.

'The feather, yes, more or less. Is there a lot of wind where you are?'

It doesn't matter. Everything's fine. There's wind and sun and the kids are playing behind their new house that has a pool while I go back to the wake with Brenda's order to hug my parents for her. I catch Dad first; he's listening to Ale's songs with Uncle Jaime next to the speakers. For a while we practically dance to the rhythm of a song sprinkled with an Andean flute that Alejandro will write on the Inca trail with Dad, almost ten years ago. Then Jaime will latch onto us and stick his big belly between us and the three of us will end up with our arms around each other's shoulders with our heads together, like athletes conspiring.

The boys must still be playing, or maybe they're eating ice cream and sitting on the edge of the pool, when I hug Mum. She's come over holding Amor by the arm to tell us that the procession is about to leave, and it's time to get into the cars.

Is it on the way to the cemetery that I feel, for the first time, the need to write about all of this? In the car from the funeral home, empty except for my grandmother and me in the backseat?

'That's it, I've seen everything now,' she says as the car starts to move.

She is ninety-one years old and she knows by heart the birthdays of her three children, seventeen grandchildren and twenty-five great-grandchildren. She dyes her hair a very light blond, and since it's short and fairly sparse, it fills with light when the sun falls on it.

It's a brief trip to the cemetery, no more than three kilometres, and that's where I decide to write about Alejandro. There or a little later, as I go with my grandmother to the cemetery chapel where Ale's casket is already waiting, placed on the proscenium. Just ahead of us walks Catalina, who buried her little sister in this same place not long ago, and who is now losing both her uncle and her guitar teacher. She walks with her head down and her hands in her trouser pockets, a few steps behind, Mauro and Mariela.

I point out to Grandma Amor that the feather came too. And it's true: the feather is resting on top of the coffin in the same spot as before, the same feather on the coffin that's now completely closed. How did they keep it from flying away?

'Don't even think about taking it off,' she says.

After Alejandro, Grandma Amor is next to cross over to the other side, in August, a month after turning ninety-two. The third death in the family in less than a year and a half: Milena at one end, Amor at the other. Milena dying in Mariela's arms as she sings her a song; Amor in the arms of her daughter Soledad, who cries and is the mother of Alejandro, who is going to die three hundred kilometres from everyone, stolen away in a magenta-coloured electrical storm.

Amor takes a seat in the first row. With a motion of my hand I excuse myself: Mum requires my presence outside. I'm the last one to join. Dad, Marcos and Mariela are listening to Mum, who wants to finish organising the afternoon.

'The first one who wants to say a few words is Catalina,' she says. 'Then Dad and I will speak, then the siblings, in order of age. OK?'

'And where is Cata?' asks Dad.

'She went to visit Milena,' says Mariela, pointing with her eyes in the general direction of the plot of land where, to this day, after almost an entire revolution of the sun, the baby's little body continues to dissolve.

Mariela doesn't want to speak during the service. She knows she won't be able to.

'There are still people arriving and sitting down,' says Dad. 'Stay close. Once everyone is here, we'll begin.'

The path that leads from the car park on the road to the brick chapel is crowded with people walking slowly in small groups or alone. Some carry umbrellas;

it's started to drizzle. The grass, swollen and shining from the rain, extends unbroken as far as the eye can see. There are no vertical stones or crosses or statues of any kind, just the occasional plaque placed on the ground. What you see if you look out is a well-tended English garden, with trees and mushrooms sprouting here and there like small islands. Marcos, Mariela and I move away, taking refuge under the foliage of an angel's trumpet tree at the back of the chapel.

There's not a single old tree, I say. They buried Pablo Vázquez here, and that was what, twenty years ago? The cemetery had just opened, everything had been recently planted.

Marcos takes a joint from his pocket and lights it. Holding in the smoke, then slowly exhaling air full of droplets, he says: 'Ale gave me my first joint. Ale is here. Thank you, Ale.'

Then he passes it to me and I take a deep drag and hand it back; Mariela doesn't smoke. Marcos was the closest to Ale. Because of their ages, they had shared more experiences. I tell him that if he wants to speak before me during the service, I don't mind at all. In Marcos's opinion, the order of events doesn't alter the product.

But that's not true. If someone had to write about Alejandro, it should have been him. If someone had to be in charge of his elegy, or of depicting him at all, it should be Marcos. In fact, Marcos did make a portrait of Alejandro, a ten-minute film titled *Portrait* in which Ale doesn't say anything at all; he only appears, twenty-six years old, sitting on the old sofa in the lair, getting his guitar ready to play, happy that Marcos is filming him. He sets up the computer to record, and the microphone; he puts on his headphones. His surfboards are there, hanging from the ceiling. Then there's a shot of a wave he rode in Costa Rica. Throughout, in the background, are instrumental fragments of his songs, fragments that perfectly capture the hypnotic quality of his music. Then he's standing outside in the sun, against the wall. He doesn't yet have hair down to his shoulders, but he does have the little beard and moustache. He looks at the camera for such a long time that his smile transforms. Marcos films him with the aperture open. He is momentarily saturated with light, and Alejandro's smile oscillates: it becomes natural, then self-conscious.

Wasn't speaking at funerals straight out of a Hollywood film?

Marcos takes a drag and says that Dad has written down what he's going to say – he's been taking notes since last night. And perhaps that's really when I start to write about Alejandro, in a way: the first time since his death that I start to search for words.

'It's beautiful to be on this trip with you two,' says Marcos, and he hugs Mariela first, then me.

After Mariela leaves, Marcos hands me the joint and insists I take another hit, one more. I explain I haven't had a bite to eat since yesterday, and after one hit I'm already high.

'Ale is here. You'll always find him here,' says Marcos, looking at the joint in his hands, then passing it to me.

I repeat his gesture. I look at the joint in my hand and for the first time since he died, I speak directly to Alejandro.

OK, Ale, since you're here, tell me what to say, I tell him. It's your funeral, what the hell do I say? Who are we talking to? To the people here? Are we talking to you? Should we talk about you? Should we try to talk about what you were like? Should we share some memory of you? Do I have to talk about how I feel? Do I have to say something encouraging?

'Say goodbye to him,' says Marcos. 'This is Alejandro's farewell.'

Alejandro's farewell, I whisper, expelling the smoke from my lungs and taking another drag. We're saying goodbye to you, Ale. It's now.

'And it's not going to happen again,' says Marcos.

Now is the time for details. The chapel bells ring three times, then stops. There are a lot of people standing outside under the awning, smoking or looking inside, and we head toward them. It was good to bring Ale's music to the wake, I say. We couldn't have a farewell for him without his music.

'Right. If Ale is anywhere, it's there.'

In his music and in a joint.

'How about the people?' asks Marcos. 'All the people who came? People he hadn't seen in a thousand years. Incredible. It's so perfect.'

Then I ask him if he saw the feather, and Marcos asks me what feather I'm talking about.

When we go into the chapel, I'm certain that all of this is already being written. I can almost see Alejandro writing to us from inside his closed casket, adorned with that condor or crow feather. It's Alejandro who is arranging us around him, Alejandro who shushes his friends, his family, one by one. He's trying to tell us something with all this, his death.

Marcos, sitting to my right, points to a girl kneeling in the aisle.

'That's Ana Laura, the one who was in the hut with Ale. The woman next to her is her mother.'

The mother looks uncomfortable kneeling. She is the only person not looking at the coffin or the cross or in our general direction. She is looking immediately around her, as though making sure she hasn't invaded anyone's space. Her daughter, long brown hair, blue dress, doesn't look even twenty-five. Her eyes are on the ceiling beams, smiling eyes like those of a blind person, as if she were hearing something funny, feeling something funny on her skin.

The Hollywood moment ends quickly, and it's emotional. Mum and Dad go up first to stand at the microphone. The audience keeps them from breaking down. I don't remember what Dad said. I remember him taking a piece of paper from his shirt pocket, I remember him unfolding it and then thinking better of it, refolding the paper and putting it in his trouser pocket. But Mum is the first to speak. She takes off her dark glasses, and her beautiful eyes – Arabian like mine – are flashing like firebolts. She thanks the assembled people over and over for having made her feel, within this immense sadness, within the greatest sadness she has ever felt, the love they had for Alejandro, the incorrigibly happy son she has just lost.

I wasn't expecting people to applaud after each speaker, but that's what they do. We even hear cheers and words of encouragement from the back of the room. When Cata finishes saying her piece, the explosion of noise is so loud that she has to cover her ears, and she stands looking out at the congregation with her brow furrowed. I guess they must clap and shout at what I say, but I'm not paying attention. I have a buzzing in my ears as I return to my seat, and my legs are still shaking, and all I can do is think back over each of the words I've just said. Now they strike me as a string of pretentious idiocies, though I believed them when I said them.

I talked about 'Wherever You Go', Ale's song that I'd had in my head when I got up that morning. I'd criticised it the first time he played it for me.

'Wherever you go, your home is inside.' It had seemed like too easy a thing to say, a pompous phrase. I'd told him so. I remember asking him if he had found his inner home, and I remember the way he sat looking at me. What I wanted to make him see was a question of ethics: to say something, you have to first embody it. Finding your inner home meant that you would never again feel alone, never again feel helpless. At least, that was how I understood it. It was like being enlightened or becoming realised, and I thought Ale seemed far from reaching that point.

That episode is what had come to my mind as I approached the microphone. That, and how Ale listened to me or pretended to listen whenever I critiqued his lyrics, and how he never changed a thing. We'd discuss them, but he'd prefer to leave even grammatical errors exactly as they were. And in my mind, the two things came together that afternoon. I'd accused him of being stubborn, but maybe Ale really didn't feel any pressure to conform to anyone. Maybe he really had made peace with his imperfection, so long as it was his own. Maybe that's what it meant to find your inner home. Maybe I was the arsehole, waiting for my house to be perfect before I could begin to inhabit it, when the only certain thing was that it would never be ready enough. Maybe that was the difference. For Alejandro, joy meant not wasting the chance to live in his house while he was building it, even if it was missing a wall or the roof was full of leaks. And Ale wasn't exactly in a hurry. Nor did he want to make it out of overly complex materials. He built it with what he had at hand, knowing that one day the wind was going to end up knocking it down like everything else. All this occurred to me there, in the little cemetery chapel, and it was what I said when it was my turn to speak. To finish, I wished him happy travels, as if I really trusted or believed that Ale was in transit toward some other place.

I can only start to really write about Alejandro when I start to write about myself. When I finally sit down to write, around mid-March, all that comes out are feelings or memories that go nowhere. Until suddenly, I remember what Mum said that morning about why it had to be Alejandro who died, when he so loved life, and I wrote ten pages in one sitting about a guy who got jealous about his brother's death. The guy felt that his younger brother, by dying first, had robbed him of a privilege. In a way, he had usurped him. By law, it was older brothers who had to go through everything first, including death. Now the younger brother had become the older one, and there was no going back.

That was going to be the tone: ironic. Ironic but not really, because it was totally true – I was going to be the first to want to die. I was going to have my chance at nineteen. I was going to spend a whole night alone in the house with Dad's revolver and three grams of coke. It'll be summer, and the rest of the family will be in La Paloma. I thought my death would be a kind of gift to my parents. I thought it was just what they needed to shake off their existential lethargy: the death of a child. But cowardice or intelligence will win out. I'm not going to shoot myself. I'm going to fire the bullet with my name on it into the sky, and some months later, when I start to feel another fit coming on – that's when I'm going to become a writer.

I'll buy a notebook with Goofy on the cover, and I'll set about writing down everything I do from one second to the next. I'm going to write at the breakfast table, on the bus, in the bathroom. I'll bring my notebook everywhere, terrified that a single thought might escape me. Half the things I write down won't have happened, they'll be pure invention, and soon my life will jumble together with the story of a kid my age who lives in a house like mine, teaches English to pay for his drugs and writes all day to occupy his hands with something less solitary than hanging himself from a beam. It's clear that the character of that book, which will end up being called *Mosh*, isn't me. He doesn't find himself angry as a bull in the scummiest dive bars on Saturday mornings, or in the cabarets pretending to be a tourist, or picking up transvestites in the doorway of Metropolis. He's an only child, and although he'll have my face at first, his entire physical being will change as the pages go by, until all that's left of me are his height, his bow legs and his sexual angst.

The plot of *Mosh* is simple: the boy's father goes to Brazil for a religious conference and leaves him in charge of his sick mother for a week, and in those seven days he lets her die. He cuts off her medication, and once she's dead, he penetrates her sexually. Though it's true that the mother in the book isn't mine, I will still hesitate. I have no way of knowing whether what I'm writing will see the light of day, but I remember reasoning that if my mother were to ever read that scene, she would be destroyed. What will convince me to go ahead is the clear understanding that if I omit something for fear of my mother's reaction, I'm going to end up sinking entirely into speciousness. I'm also going to be afraid of Dad's reaction, and I'll imagine coming to blows with him, but it's write or die. If I can't be free in my writing,

I tell myself, I won't be able to be free anywhere. As I write, I discover that I can expel my parents from the domains they'd conquered with impunity since my early childhood. That idea gives me the extra energy I need when my mind falters and my attention, so focused on the objects around me and the anxieties of my body, threatens to falter and the words start to lose meaning on the page. When the propulsion comes to an end, it will be obvious. After I set down the text's final full stop, I will be left in shock. I will have something in my hands that has separated from me, and it will be like a book, and I will be a different person.

I reproached my parents for being Mormons, for filling my head with all that Mormon shit from the day I was born, pure shit, repressive and false. From the outside, as far as anyone could see, my parents hadn't been abusive to me or any of my siblings. In any case, they had been more attentive with their children than most of my friends' parents had, much more loving. I remember I lost almost all my friends when the book came out. They adored my parents. They would have liked to have parents like mine. They thought my negativity was an act. They thought I was groundlessly complaining, that my madness wasn't sincere, that it was an excuse. And maybe they weren't far off. Maybe I fell in love with misery. Maybe I had to invent myself some misery so I could seem interesting, play the *poète maudit*. Maybe I was creating my own myth and starting to believe it. Maybe that misery was my first fiction.

It didn't happen overnight. I gradually rejected the church as I started opening up to things outside it, at seventeen, and my parents started to pile on me with their interminable sermons. Irate sermons, unfair sermons, but sermons that were at least partially justified, because their loss wasn't just any loss: it was a cosmic one. As Christians, they believed in personal salvation, the possibility of eternal life for every individual; but as Mormons, they also believed in the salvation of the family group. They believed that the family, composed of father, mother and children, could come back to life and live together forever, all converted into gods. That was the loss I was inflicting on my parents with my disavowal. They'd had children so those children would live forever. With them, all together, for eternity, as gods.

'Don't you want to live with us forever?'

Absurdly, that's the mantra they'll use in their attempts to sway me. Their sermons will take place in my room, and after hours of sobbing and begging the place will be infected by the ghosts of betrayal and failure.

They'll ask me to set myself straight, to return to the church, to do it for my younger siblings, who will be inclined to follow my example. They didn't know what it was to grow up in the church. They didn't know the poisonous effects it could have. They had chosen it as adults. And although I was the young one and they the ones who had once been teenagers, they asked me to try to understand them.

'Try to understand us,' they will tell me, and I, in a way, will obey them. I'm going to spend the rest of my life trying to understand them. I'm going to become a writer to try to understand them.

'Everything we did was with the best of intentions,' they said when I reproached them for all the rubbish they'd filled my head with. 'Doesn't that count for anything?'

My suicide, I figure, would only have confirmed their idea that I'd gone down the wrong path. If I'd killed myself, maybe all of them, my parents and my siblings, would today be tethered more firmly than ever to the church and its fantastical agenda. I like to think that's why I don't blow my brains out that night when I'm nineteen: because I sense that only by continuing with my life will I manage to extract my siblings from the moral ruin of the monster factory. I'm going to assume that responsibility after having discovered that the road to perdition is, to say the least, much more real than the other.

And in fact, in a few years, after I've become a published writer, there won't be a single Mormon left in the house. Mariela will get pregnant out of wedlock at twenty-three. At sixteen, Ale is going to start dating Agustina and will be the last to deal with religious-hued sermons – already fainter than the ones I was dealt, because my parents' faith will be nearly extinguished by then. They've lost two children irrevocably (at thirteen, Marcos is still too little to be lost or found), and rather than live for all eternity as gods in Mormon heaven – gods with a permanent and terrible pain – they're going to leave the church. They're going to choose to jump ship behind their progeny, and they'll start to live out in the open, with a vast horizon drawing ever closer.

Mum is going to toy with the idea of returning to the church, though she admits she has lost the ability to believe. She would return for the friendships, for the sense of community and because in the church, whether she believes or not, she could still do humanitarian work. Fortunately, her heart or the little voice of her conscience won't allow her to deceive herself a second time; she's no longer as naïve as she was at twenty-three, when she and my father agreed to let their brains be washed. What was the moment of that decision like? What was it like, the instant when you decide to surrender and sacrifice your intelligence and accept a rulebook as a replacement for your inner life? Inner life, if it *was* life, was unpredictable; it never stopped moving. I understood the wish for it to all stay still, even if just for a second, but from there to the desire for it to dry up completely was a leap that my mind couldn't make, and when I think of my parents succumbing so young it fills me with rage and sorrow – a sorrow that leads inevitably to rage – because with the best of intentions they'll end up injecting all of their fear and insanity into us. Because everything I write at first will be a document of my parents' madness and a document of my misery. And because my talent for writing and my misery, both of which will make me so proud, had been fertilised and refined by that madness I'll so desperately need, and from which in the end, sadly, I will also suffer.

More or less from the time Mariela finished secondary school, they had acquired the strange habit of constantly telling us about their own parents. They were like small children when they did it. They couldn't talk about their parents without falling all over themselves with praise. They held them up as examples of self-abnegation. I was sure that my grandparents had emphasised ad nauseam the unpayable debt their children owed, because when my parents would list all the efforts they were making to raise us, it was clear that they were repeating, word for word, the phrases they'd heard from my grandparents. Not only that: they'd also speak with the same emphasis, the same intonation, the same fury. That's where everything had started for them, too. When would the chain be broken?

During the day, when they're home, the only thing I do is lock myself in my room to write, especially on weekends. On Saturdays, after recovering from the previous night's partying, I'll stay in bed all day – or sometimes I'll camp out on the roof so I can smoke in peace while I write my second book – and I won't emerge until Monday morning when I go to work. They won't worry about my seclusion. Every time they open my door they'll see me writing. They will ask me what I'm working on and I'll tell them stories, novels; they won't know I'm planting time bombs in our model family. They won't know that when I write that scene of necrophilic incest, unconcerned about the repercussions, I will be inaugurated as a writer, and now there are no limits to what I can write.

My strategy isn't going to work, though at first it will seem like it does. *Mosh* and *Melt* will be published almost simultaneously, only a month apart. And on the rare night when I sit watching TV in the living room instead of writing in my room, who is going to emerge from the hallway in a nightgown if not Mum, practically crawling, her hair frizzy, my books in her hand.

The first thing she asks me is what she and Dad did wrong for me to have something so monstrous inside me. And I'm going to feel something between perplexed and triumphant, trying to calibrate the size of the wound that begins to ooze out of her mouth, amazed at her monstrous appearance in the light of the TV. It will all be intensified by the strange absence of my father, who will stay in the bedroom just a few metres away, not making a sound. Does he stay in his room listening to it all because he's afraid we'll otherwise come to blows? Could it be that he understands me? My answer to my mother that night will be simple: better out than in, I'll tell her.

You should be happy I've been able to put all that on paper. It's why I'm alive.

'How could you treat us like that in your books?' she will ask me, moving as if to sit down on the other end of the sofa, then deciding to stay standing. 'Why are you doing this to me? How could you do that to your mother? You portray me as sick. And then you practically kill her, and then... it's horrible. I swear I can't understand.'

I'm going to tell her that characters aren't people, that there's no need to be psychotic and confuse fantasy with reality.

'Are you calling me psychotic? Are you calling *us* psychotic?' she'll say, raising her voice, rolling her eyes in the direction of the hallway, which remains silent. 'Why write something like that? If you have talent, if you have a gift, why not use it to write something that edifies people, lifts them up? Do you realise what you wrote?'

I'm going to try to explain to her that they're all metaphors. The son in the book lets the mother die so she won't be sick anymore and will stop suffering, and then he has relations with her to bring her back to life, to have a new mother. Sex is a symbol of life. It's art, let's not get confused.

She's going to withdraw, leaving my books on the armchair, murmuring that they aren't art. That isn't art, that isn't art, she'll say. The reigning tension of those days will be completely transformed when the two-page reviews start to arrive in droves, the covers of cultural supplements, the TV and radio interviews, the publications abroad. Instantly, as though by magic, I will go from being her son the monster to her son the writer, and my books' poisonous power will be reduced practically to zero.

All of these things, which I believed had been buried for a long time, come back with unexpected force in the days following Alejandro's death. I don't remember what it was that led me to tell my parents that I'd started to write about Ale. I do remember that we were in the kitchen of their house, where most of our conversations take place.

My father thinks it's a good thing. It's good for me to have catharsis if I need it.

'Art arises from pain, right, Dani?' he says, outlining an argument I'd convinced him of after my first books, when I was starting to be considered an artist. In fact, I had convinced myself of that; it was one of the arguments that had most fascinated me while I prepared for my first interviews by reading writer profiles in *El País Cultural*, in *V de Vian*, and in back issues of *The Paris Review* I found at the Tristán Narvaja street market. Many authors, if not most, said they started writing out of their pain, out of a loss of some kind. Ricardo had always said the same. Ricardo talked about how art flowed from a wound. Loss always brought a revelation; I'd never been able to forget that concept.

'I don't like you writing about us,' says Mum.

I tell her not to worry. In what I was writing almost no one says what they'd really said or does what they had done. Plus, everyone has different names. And instead of five siblings, as in real life, in the book there are four. I've had to divide Pablo, the middle one, among the others.

What's more, I'm not actually writing about them – I'd need a separate book for that, I joke. It's about Ale and about death, though it isn't really about Ale either. It isn't a biography. I couldn't write a book trying to show what Alejandro had been like. He'd been the most beautiful baby my mother had ever seen – that, for example, I could say. That detail was going to have to be there: it was the start of his legend, just like mine was having had the biggest head, so big I almost couldn't get out, while Mariela had been a black ball of hair, and Marcos had been born with his eyes open. Ale had also been the first sibling to make me feel grown up. I remember a photograph that must have been in an album somewhere. I remember the moment when they'd taken that photo: me on the sofa holding Ale. He couldn't have been more than a month old and he was lying on my lap, his head resting on my elbow, which I raised a little to act as a pillow. I remembered how big I'd felt at that moment, the seriousness I felt. Ale was that. I could tell it, but that wasn't all Ale was.

'Then what is your book going to be?' Mum wants to know, before I carry on with my vagaries.

Since I don't have an answer, I tell her that it isn't unusual for a writer's family to appear, more or less disguised, in his texts. Writers who don't write about their families, particularly about their parents, tend to be bad writers, I tell them. They don't have to write directly about their parents, but parental figures need to hang over their literature in some way. It's a good sign when that happens. Parents, grandparents, whoever it was who'd raised them. In Borges they appear all the time. When they appear in Hemingway, it's moving, like in Carver. When their shadows loom in Kafka, it's terrifying. But maybe it's necessary to wait until the parents are dead in order to really write about them, I'm not sure. The death of parents seems to have a special effect on their children, especially on writer children.

Since it's relevant, I tell them about what had happened to a writer friend of mine. She'd had a strange relationship with her parents, who were old and infirm. She was single, past child-bearing age, and she lived with them in the apartment where she'd grown up. In their final stage, she'd been their nurse. Her parents' illnesses were different, and she'd had to exchange the double bed for a couple of twin beds in order to attend to them correctly. Around that time she'd published a novel, a good novel, an entertaining, ingenious, fatally boring novel. But the central chapter was a masterpiece. It was a nightmare that the protagonist had. The writing took a quantum leap. It acquired an intensity and a feeling of risk that belonged to a different book. I asked her where that text had come from and why she didn't write more things like that, and she replied that her parents read everything she published and she didn't want to hurt them. And it was true: in the nightmare there was a little girl, a lot of snakes, some blurry paternal figures. That nightmare she'd written involved her parents, and it was the moment when her writing had really taken flight. In my opinion it was a clear sign that she should continue in that direction, but she thought it was wrong to write about one's parents. She said that most autobiographical writers wrote to get revenge on their loved ones, especially their parents. She thought the most decent thing, the bravest thing, was to solve problems by talking them through in person. Although she didn't admit it, she must have felt a kind of vertigo when she wrote that nightmare. She had to know that she was eventually going to have to write about those things, and that that's how her writing would be saved. I imagined her taking care of her father and mother, giving them medicine, bathing them, wishing deep down that they would die once and for all so she could finally get to work. But the parents' death is no guarantee, either. My friend's parents had indeed finally died, with a couple of months between them, and instead of feeling liberated when she set out to write about them, she suffered the opposite effect. She continued to refuse to write about her father and mother, more firmly now than ever. Now that they were dead and couldn't defend themselves, it struck her as the worst immorality there was; it was a question of dignity, of respect.

When I was twenty-three, *Melt* was published in Spain, and then negotiations over a French translation began, though they never bore fruit. It was a very modest success, but it was enough to change my situation completely. I'll be hired as a fiction reviewer for *Insomnia*, the cultural supplement of the magazine *Posdata*, and I'll also work as a bartender four nights a week at El Ciudadano, and I'm going to be able to cut the classes I teach at the Anglo down to the bare minimum. I'm going to feel like a prodigy, and I'll want to express some of that feeling in my writing. I'm going to want to write something luminous, and I'm going to fail spectacularly, entering a nervous state that will keep me up for me several nights in a row. One day, while I'm smoking a cigarette on the roof, it will dawn on me that everything I've written, I've written there, in my childhood home. I will decide that I'll only be able to definitively leave that darkness behind when I escape my parents' aura, and in less than two weeks I will have rented an apartment in the Old City.

It will be a noisy, interior apartment, but it will be *my* place, the rules will be *mine,* and no sooner do I install the computer than I start writing *November*, my third novel, which opens with an image that has been hounding me for some time: a man and a woman in the garden of a beach house in the moments before sunrise.

Soon I'll discover it's a memory that the man in the relationship, Guzmán, is recalling as he sits at table in a bar one Friday night. Guzmán is separated from his wife and struggling to cope with the separation, and there's a daughter in the mix: Maite. The next day, Saturday, Guzmán is going to pick her up at her mother's house. The first ten, twelve pages describe those Saturday hours that father and daughter will spend together. There is sunlight, they go down to the beach, have a barbecue, take a nap, play. Later, when night comes, they lay down to sleep in his bed.

The book will be melancholic in tone, but I'm going to have faith in the material. A young couple struggling to survive in difficult times. It's going to be a love story. Lost love, love recovered. Romantic love, filial love. There will be pain, there will be conflict, but I won't succumb to my habitual darkness and pessimism. I'll be encouraged by the fact that the story is coming out in the third person, which has never happened before, and I'm going to take it as confirmation that I am maturing.

With no advance warning, Maite dies. The father wakes up on Sunday morning and finds her dead beside him. I'm going to refuse to write it and I'll spend some time away from the novel, battling the depression I feel when I see how my mind is taking the same tortured path as always. I'll think: if I want to explore new territory, I'm going to have to hang in there and not cede to the first impulse. I'm going to distance myself from the novel in hopes that the story will head in other directions without me. But every time I return to my desk, I'll find the dead girl still there.

No sooner do I move than I start to write, and I also start seeing Sandra. There won't be any feelings between us. She's the first customer from the bar I go to bed with; she'll be my first married woman, a mother, older than I am (twenty-nine). I'm her first infidelity, and her nerves always get the better of her excitement and feed my own. I've been stuck for over a month on *November* when Sandra loses her son Miguel (four) in a car accident. There's a Disco supermarket three blocks from their house and they always walk to it, but this time, at the boy's request, the father takes him in the car while Sandra stays home baking some scones to eat in the evening. It's the boy who asks the father if he can ride in the passenger seat and the father, contrary to habit, against his instincts and against the agreement he has with Sandra, agrees. A delivery truck, going more than eighty kilometres an hour, drives into them on the corner of Libertad and Soca. Miguel flies through the windscreen and dies immediately. I'm going to hear some of the details from Sandra herself in the morgue, just a couple of hours later.

When she calls me, I'm chatting with some students in the courtyard of the Anglo. It will be barely five and I'll have just one class left. Under normal conditions I'm usually desperate to get home early, but with my writer's block I'll prefer instead to wear myself out on aimless walks, to hide out in a cinema, to have a drink somewhere, and I'll only go home when I've found a solution to the text, or, in the worst case, when I stop caring. I'm going to be considering my options for the rest of the afternoon when I get Sandra's call. Aside from the shock of the news, I'm going to be surprised that she would call me about something like this. Her voice sounds slow when she asks me if I can come and be with her.

Why was she calling me? Don't you have friends? I ask her over the phone. Don't you have family? I ask.

When I reach the morgue, I find myself soaked in a cold sweat. I don't remember how I got there. I don't remember a single red light. I will have driven over ten kilometres and the only thing I'll remember is the chorus of a *cumbia* that repeats incessantly through the entire drive.

> *You shouldn't have toyed with my foolish heart.*
> *Someday, I know, you'll pay for that.*
> *Do you think you're a goddess, a star?*
> *Someday, my pretty petal, you'll also die.*

108

My first impression, maybe because of how inhospitable the hallway is, will be that Sandra has shrunk to half her size. She's alone except for one other woman who is holding her hand. The woman will look me up and down while Sandra walks toward me, and as she tells me about the accident, whispering in my ear and vaguely motioning toward a door at the end of the hall, where I gather that her son's body is lying. Then, in an even quieter voice that only I can hear, now looking directly at me and trying to read my reactions, she'll tell me she always knew that little Miguel was going to die.

'I've known ever since he was born. Don't ask me how, and don't think I'm out of my mind,' she'll say, 'but I had to tell someone. No one else can know and no one else will ever know. Do you know what kind of torture it is to spend four years knowing he's going to die? Do you know what it's like to live with that terror every day? Do you believe what I'm telling you? But now it's done. Now I don't have to be afraid anymore.'

I remember a commotion and then being surrounded by people, and I slip away through them. I'll find a door a little further down that leads to an inner patio, and I'm going to smoke there for a while, one foot in and one foot out, feeling translucent, looking at the windows on the other side of the patio and studying a section of the wall across from me; a few of the tiles are coming off and someone has tried to stick them back on with adhesive tape. I'll be about to leave when little Miguel's father appears on the arm of an old lady who is almost as tall as he is. When the man sees Sandra, he breaks down. They have to help him sit down on a bench. Sandra kneels down in front of him and tries to snap him out of it, lifting his chin and talking to him, but the guy is going to cover his ears and close his eyes, squeezing his eyelids as tightly as he can.

While the guy shakes his head and his nose starts to run, I know two things: that I'm never going to speak to Sandra again, and that I'm going to start writing as soon as I get home. First, when I step out onto the sidewalk, I nearly collide with a public phone. A woman in a hat who'd been smoking outside changes a bill for coins, and I call my mother's house. When Mum answers, her voice makes me start to cry. She asks me what's wrong, and I say I just needed to hear her voice. I tell her that the son of a friend of mine has died in an accident. She doesn't ask for many details.

'How terrible,' she says, but she doesn't depress me. It's good for me to feel her sadness, and how at the same time she's happy I've called. She lets me hear her for a good while. I only perceive the sound of her voice, and I don't remember what else she said to me, except that I should calm down and support my friend. But what I actually do is drive home unhurriedly, feeling the novel taking shape in my head.

The image of Miguel's father – that big man who wanted to shut out the world – is what will give me the key to the rest of the book. The same thing will happen to Guzmán, the father in the novel. He won't be able, won't want to look at his dead daughter, and so I'm not going to have to describe her. When the guy wakes up and sees that his daughter isn't breathing, he will be unable to look at her, and everything will start to happen as though it's happening around her and her body, invisible without the father's gaze. My only function will be to follow that father, focus in on his floundering mind, and let my reluctance to look at the cadaver be his.

While I'm writing the book, I'm going to feel dirty, as if Sandra had left my body coated in grime, a muck that will inform my novel. I won't feel that she's far away from me. In fact, as I take advantage of her tragedy for

110

my book, I'm going to feel her presence so close by that I'll be forced to take refuge in the most pitiless corners of my soul. I'll write, again, as Ricardo used to say, from a hardness of heart, from the cold. I'll end up plunging into a pit of superstition, thinking that there's a strange connection between the death of her son and the death of the girl in the novel, wondering what would have happened if, instead of putting it off, I had decided to kill the girl in the novel in due time and in the right way. Every so often I am absolutely convinced that if I'd killed her in time, Sandra's son wouldn't have had to die. And then there's the fact that Guzmán, the father in the novel, also lets his daughter sit in the front seat of the car when he goes to collect her from her mother's house. The girl in the novel doesn't die in an accident, but she does die beside her father, a victim of his negligence.

I'm going to experience a vague remorse when I don't answer her calls, of which there won't be more than two or three. I'll be paranoid for a while, but fortunately – out of decorum or something else – Sandra won't return to my house or to El Ciudadano. There will be times, however, when I want to see her, feeling an unhealthy curiosity to know how everything is going and to give it to her up the arse until she can't take it anymore. I'll be haunted by her eyes and her voice in the morgue. I will wonder: how could it be that there wasn't the slightest sign of horror in her eyes? How could it be that she sounded relieved and completely in her right mind? Will there be honesty – a terrifying one, but honesty nonetheless – in admitting that her fear was hope? At some point, I'll tell myself, the darkness of it all is going to catch up with Sandra. Sooner or later, it's going to swallow her. Or maybe not: maybe she can live out the rest of her life relieved, validated and at peace. In any case, I'm not going to be there when any of those things happen.

Out of the confusion that will plague me during that period, I'll gradually distil a theory that dawns on me all of a sudden thirteen years later, the morning of 9th February, when I watch Mum and Dad receive the news of Alejandro's death, in the lair. They look stunned at how familiar they find the scene, and by the idea, still silent, that they've been practicing for this their whole lives. They know exactly what to say.

This is the worst thing that could have happened to them.

It's what Mum says, bringing her hands to her face, as if the mask she'd been wearing was coming to life now, just as the performance was starting, just as it was beginning to smother her. Dad expresses it in his own way a few hours later, after he comes back from Playa Grande, when he says that it's his fault, that Ale was living the life he himself had given up. The next day, when the funeral is over and we're back at their house, dusk falling, Dad indicates he's seeing his own hand ever more clearly in the moment's oneiric weave.

'I called him all the time about those storms,' says my father. 'I was worried. I knew that idiot went to the lifeguard hut sometimes. He told me not to worry, that if he could he always went to Canary's or Dwarf's. But I thought about it a lot, more than usual these past few days. I was really anxious. I told him not to be an idiot, not to go out there. Do you think I could have pushed him to go by telling him not to?'

'Oh, Miguel,' says Mum. 'Alejandro wasn't a little kid you forbid from touching the plug socket and then he goes and touches it.'

'It's odd that I would feel so afraid recently,' says Dad.

But they were always afraid something would happen to us. We're in the same living room where, at nineteen years old, almost nineteen years ago, I'm going to flirt with the idea of self-elimination. Mum is in Dad's rocking chair; instead of facing the TV as usual, she's turned toward my father, who is standing next to the heater. At a certain point, around the middle of my adolescence, the chimney is going to get clogged and it will start spitting out smoke, and the wood fire will be substituted with a gas apparatus whose ceramic exterior looks like a stack of logs. Then, with the arrival of the cooling and heating system, the heater will be relegated to a purely decorative role. Today, there's also an old iron pot in the fireplace, and a sky-blue wooden trunk where my mother keeps toys she buys so my sons can play when we come to visit.

From my armchair I ask Dad what he's most afraid of. He replies that it's this, that something bad will happen to us.

And before? I ask. Before you were married and had children? Because you weren't always husband and wife and you weren't always someone's parents. What were you afraid of before? Dying?

'I don't know if it was of dying,' he says. 'Maybe it was fear of dying, yes, but more of suffering, I think. More than anything it was fear of suffering, or of being left alone.'

'Fear of pain, but also of dying,' says Mum. 'Everyone is afraid of dying.'

'Not exactly of dying,' says Dad. 'But of dying without having lived, without having found the truth.'

All fears come true. I say it thinking of Sandra. Seeing her as the architect of her little boy's death is going to strike me as a pretentious idea, a morbid distortion, but in the logic of the night – my writing time when I live

113

in the Old City – I'll have no doubt at all that the world is always going to conspire with our most hidden parts, offering up the raw materials for us to enact our most private nightmares.

'So then what should we do?' asks Dad. He looks around as though searching for an escape route from the dream he's waking from.

How was I to know? Stop being afraid? Could a person stop being afraid?

'Can we?' my father seconded. 'Can we stop being afraid?'

'You're always going to be afraid,' says Mum. 'If you love life, you're not going to want to die. The fear can only leave you if you die. Then you aren't afraid, you don't have anything anymore. You don't feel fear or love or anything. I'd rather be dead than live without feeling anything.'

If you think of it like that, everything is tragedy, I say.

'It is. It's a tragedy. The worst thing that can happen to anyone is to have a child die,' she says. 'Losing a child is the worst thing that can happen, and that's why you're afraid of it. Aren't you afraid of dying? Aren't you afraid of something happening to your children?'

I'm terrified for Paco and I don't know what to do. I only know I don't want to have that fear anymore, because it's horrible. If Paco gets the flu, a sore throat, whatever, I go crazy. I get angry. I get angry at him. What do I achieve with that? Nothing, I just make him feel worse than he already does. Now the poor kid is turning into a hypochondriac. He comes to tell me about the slightest pain. And he has a strange way of describing his aches. Instead of saying his head hurts, he says he has a pain in his forehead, and it makes me imagine tumours, aneurysms.

'But why Paco?' Mum asks me.

It doesn't matter why Paco. All I want is to get rid of the fear. We already know we're going to die, I say. We already know that no one gets out alive. Even if you won't be there to see it, everyone's going to die anyway. But why do they have to die a thousand times in my head first? I can't take it anymore. I want them to stop dying in my head. Has it always been like this? How long have children died their first thousand deaths in the heads of their parents?

'That's natural. The more you love someone, the more afraid you are that you'll have to lose them. All the parents in the world are afraid their children will die. A parent's love for their children is the greatest love possible.'

How did she know that it was all parents? Had she talked to all of them? Maybe there was one who wasn't like that.

'There are lots of them, Dani. More than there should be, unfortunately. How many fathers and mothers are out there who don't care about their children and abandon them, mistreat them, abuse and neglect them?'

I didn't mean that. I meant that there has to be a father in the world who isn't afraid of his children's death, but still loves them. I'd have liked to be that one.

'You want to be special,' says Mum.

But isn't the worst thing, really, when your fears come true? Isn't that the worst? When you've been afraid of something every day of your life and suddenly it happens? You start to wonder whether maybe you'd had something to do with it. You start to suspect that maybe all your concentrated fear had made something happen. The suspicion, that's the worst thing.

'That's what I was talking about,' says Dad. 'That's what I was wondering. If we didn't... if I didn't have something to do with Ale's death... I don't know if these are things a person can think. They're difficult. No one knows what it's like.'

That's when Mum explodes. She can't believe what she's hearing.

'If it were down to us, Ale would still be alive!' she says. 'If we could have, we would have got him out of that damned hut! If God would allow it, I'd be dead now, not him…!'

Then she accuses me of being like a little kid who blames his parents for everything.

Not a little kid, I tell her; a teenager. But all of us here are like little kids, I say then. No one knows anything about anything, I say. We don't know anything about death, and that's why we don't know even half of what there is to know about life. All I was saying was that it would be best to get all those fears out of our heads.

'But how?' asks Dad.

Talking is something, I say. Talking is a start.

'Yes, we have to talk,' agrees Dad. 'But talking is so hard.'

'Talking doesn't solve anything,' says Mum.

'How could we not talk, Sole?' he asks her. 'Sole, love, we have to be able to talk…'

'Talking is how you end up hurting people,' she says.

Then Dad asks if he can tell us about the dream he had. He asks it shyly, a shining layer of wetness in his eyes.

'I want to tell you. I can't keep it in anymore.'

'What are you going to say, Miguel?'

'I had a dream the night Ale died. It was so powerful it woke me up. It was already light outside.'

'You didn't tell me,' says Mum.

In the dream, Dad is standing in the kitchen of my house in Parque del Plata, looking toward the living room where a wooden hut is burning. Dad can't move for as long as the dream lasts, nor can he do anything to put out the fire or sound the alarm. It's an intense fire, red and orange, that burns on its own. The flames don't spread to the curtains or the furniture, but the scene distresses him. Then I appear: I come out of my room like someone getting up in the middle of the night to drink a glass of water, and I stop short when I see the flames.

'You stopped when you saw the bonfire,' says Dad. 'Then you realised I was there too. You looked at me, and the dream ended there.'

Mum snorts and gets up from the rocking chair saying she's going to her room. Dad tries to stop her.

'Don't leave, Sole,' he said. 'Don't make me feel bad about a dream.'

But she doesn't want to talk anymore.

'You can have all the dreams you want,' she tells him. 'I want to be alone.'

After Mum closes the door, Dad's disappointment doesn't take long to dissipate, partly because of Mariela's arrival; she'd been in the lair with Marcos.

'Come on in, we're talking,' Dad tells her.

Mariela pours a glass of water and drinks it as she listens to her father's dream.

'Can you believe it?' Dad asks us. 'What was a wooden hut doing in Dani's house? A hut that was on fire – don't you think it's strange?'

Mariela has her hands on her hips. She shakes her head, then bows it. 'You knew he was dying.'

'Is that it?' asks Dad. 'But Ale wasn't in the dream.'

'But one of your sons was. Dani was there, it's the same thing,' says Mariela. 'In dreams, things aren't what they are.'

'Could it be? Did I know Ale was dying? Was it a premonition?'

But maybe Dad dreamed about me because in the back of his mind he expected me to be the one to die. I say it out loud.

'How could I expect that, Dani?'

If someone told you one of your children was going to die, who would you have bet on? You'd have bet on me, right?

'Maybe.'

I think that in the back of all our minds, I was going to be the first one to die, I say. Or Mum, because of her health problems.

'It's hard to talk.'

Parque del Plata was the last house where Ale lived, in those months he spent with me after he left Lucía's. He wasn't going to return to Parque after the season at Rocha; we'd already talked about it. The two of us didn't fit in that house. Ale was too big. He took up too much space. I'd come home from work and the guy was all spread out in the living room: the instruments, the sheets of music, the amps and notebooks. He said more than once that he didn't feel like I'd kicked him out when I told him it would be best he didn't come back after the summer. Didn't he have about ten grand saved up? After the season he'd have four thousand more. He should use it. Why didn't he rent something? Or if he felt like renting was throwing money away, why not finally buy that famous piece of land in Maldonado? Years of looking at plots. I thought I was doing him a favour by telling him to look for his own place. Now, on the night of his funeral, this thought crosses my mind: what if he stopped caring about living when he found himself without a house to go back to? What if it made him depressed?

'He could always have come back here,' says Dad,

after listening to my conjecture.

Ale wasn't about to go back to the lair, especially with Maca and Marcos living in it.

'He could have stayed with us in the house, in any of the bedrooms. This is his house. It will always belong to all of you. And he didn't feel kicked out. He understood that he couldn't stay in Parque very long. It's your children's house. He respected that. Ale said you were the best father in the world, the way you treated your kids, the way you played with them.'

The idiot said that?

'He did. Ale talked to me,' says Dad. 'I want you to know. He wasn't mad at you. He was really excited about his freedom.'

I hope so. For my own good, I hope so.

'What happened was that you felt him there while you were asleep and your mind turned it into a dream and that's how it manifested, as best it could,' says Mariela.

Dad, out of nowhere, starts to cry. He doesn't even try to hold back his tears. He lets out a strange hiccup, as if he were suffocating, and then he doesn't make any more noise, just lets the tears fall. He says it's a miracle. His lips are wet with tears as he brings a hand to his nose, which has started to run.

'It's a miracle,' he repeats, 'and at the same time it's the most natural thing. The dream, what happened today at the funeral. It's the most natural thing in the world to have these perceptions. It's a miracle. What I had was a dream. It was psychological, a biochemical signal, the unconscious – call it whatever the hell you want, but it's a miracle.'

'We have to try not to put so much mysticism into it,' says Mariela, her voice suddenly hoarse. 'We have to keep calm and not try to find a mystical angle to it all...'

'It's a miracle that a connection could be so deep,' says

my father. 'It's a strange feeling. There's almost no sadness in it. There's not. Sadness is a word. If I think about it, I feel guilty for not being sad right now. Even Mum felt it during the funeral, did you hear what she said?'

Fuck guilt.

'I never would have imagined that the funeral of a child of mine would be like that. Ale's funeral. All those people. Everyone told me they'd never seen anything like it. People left with their spirit... their spirits lifted. Is it bad to say it was beautiful?' says Dad, looking fleetingly toward his bedroom, massaging his left arm.

Mariela wants to know if he feels OK.

'Are you OK, Dad? What's wrong?' she interrupts him, and she orders him to stop rubbing his arm, he's making her nervous. I encourage him. I tell him: talk, Veteran, preach as much as you like.

Mariela looks at me with rage, then takes Dad by the shoulders to guide him toward the armchair, but Dad won't move from his spot and he asks her to let him be.

'I'm OK, Mariela,' he tells her. 'I'm not going to sit. If something's going to happen to me, then let it hit me standing, dammit. Did I need Ale to die in order to realise that death doesn't exist? I don't know the half of the half of anything, but Ale isn't dead.'

He starts to laugh hard, his face twinkling with the tears that continue to fall. He roars with laughter and clutches his arm, and Mariela lowers onto the edge of the armchair, boiling inside, expecting Dad to fall over any second.

'Was this what had to happen? I understand now. I don't need any more blows. I'm OK. There's no such thing as the dead. How can they exist, when they're dead?' he says. 'Before, when I talked, I felt wise and I was an idiot. Now I hear myself speak and I sound like a crazy man, but I've never been saner in my life. How can that be? A person forgets so he can remember. Let's be crazy forever, please.'

He says it to no one, shaking his head, while his hands fumble for the armchair behind him. He leans completely back, the nape of his neck resting on the back, his legs stretched out with his heels resting on the floor, arms hanging to either side, and he clenches his hands and starts to move as if he were waking up. Then he asks me if I remember what we talked about Monday night on the porch. Of course I remember.

'What was Ale doing when we were talking about those things, Dani?' he asks me. 'Do you remember? He was leaving. Ale was leaving; he didn't care. Rockefeller or any of those monkeys, they don't matter. Only one thing matters. I don't know what it is, but it certainly isn't Rockefeller.'

'Take it easy, Dad. Drink some water,' orders Mariela, who returns from the kitchen and holds out the glass to him.

'Rockefeller,' says Dad, not looking at her. 'Poor Rockefeller. I hope he has the chance to touch these depths someday. He's the poorest man on earth. I wish it for him with all my heart. Don't let me mention his name again if I'm not praying for his soul. And Mum leaves, too. She doesn't like those conversations.'

Then Mariela asks where Mum is and in unison we say she's in her room. Dad asks her to knock first if she's going to go in, because Mum might be asleep. She wanted to be alone.

'Tell her I'll be in later,' he says.

Then, finally, the violence explodes. It doesn't take even five seconds. Mariela forgets to knock at the door before going into Mum's room. She opens the door and goes in quietly, saying Mum, Mum?

'What are you doing?' we hear her say then, once

she's in the room. 'What is this? What are you doing?'

Then we hear Mum's voice but not what she says; Mariela's rising voice drowns her out. We only hear Mum clearly when she cries for help.

'Miguel, Miguel!' she cries. 'Help, please, Miguel!'

Mum says later that Mariela raised a hand to her. Whether she actually hits her or just threatens to, I can't tell. When I get to the bedroom – before Dad, who feels dizzy when he stands up from the armchair and waves me on – Mum and Mariela are a single thing in motion at the edge of the bed. They're struggling, Mariela leaning over Mum, Mum fighting her off with a raised knee. When she sees me, Mariela lets go of Mum and steps away from her. Her arteries stand out from her neck as she yells that Mum was going through Ale's mobile phone. Mum is pressing her chest as if she were in pain, panting, and her only daughter screams at her: 'You don't do that! You just don't do it!'

I don't take part in the argument. I don't have anything to say, although Mum and Mariela insist on looking at me while they fight over who has the right to do what, and Dad tries to mediate. At a certain point Mum gets distracted, and Mariela takes the chance to grab the phone out of her hands. She immediately turns her back to ward off Mum's attack, and she tries to break Alejandro's iPhone as if it were a bar of chocolate. She ends up smashing it onto the floor. The phone doesn't break, it just has a crack in the screen after Mariela stomps on it a couple of times, the rest of us looking on in shock. The last thing I see is Dad, who bends down to pick up the mobile phone. Crouching there, he asks Mariela and me to leave them alone.

In the doorway to the lair, Marcos is playing guitar on a tree stump we sometimes use as a seat. He's sitting close to the fire he's lit on the ground next to the grill. Marcos, who never lets his hair down, is now wearing it loose, and his mouth is set in a way that looks like he's sucking on a boiled sweet, just like Alejandro used to do when he was concentrating. It made me think about Lucía's father and Lucía's father's brother.

Mariela goes straight into the lair, closing the sliding door, and starts to walk in circles, gesticulating with her arms. Then I see her talking on the phone, surely with Mauro. We can hear her over the chords Marcos is strumming, until he slams a hand on the strings to silence them and asks me what's going on. As soon as I explain, Mariela emerges from the lair. What did Mum want with that phone? That's what she wanted us to explain to her.

'What is she going to get out of looking through Ale's messages?'

According to Marcos, Mum has suspicions. She suspects Ana Laura. She'd told him so on the way back from the funeral. She doesn't think Ana Laura really has amnesia. She thinks she's hiding something.

Hadn't we agreed that he was struck by lightning? I ask, to which Marcos replies by asking Mariela to turn out the lights in the lair. When she does, the stars are right on top of us. The sky has cleared and the damp air makes them shine intensely. Mariela wonders what Ana Laura could have done to Alejandro. For a second, the cricket-filled night turns mournful.

Marcos is surprised that neither Mariela nor I had gone to talk to Ana Laura and her mother. Ana Laura suffered from the lightning. Aside from the memory loss, she has a detached retina and the base of her heel was burned. She isn't well. She's medicated.

'Her mum was nice,' he says, 'but fierce. You could

tell she was on the defensive. I don't know what she was expecting.'

I ask Marcos, as if he had any way of knowing, whether Ana Laura will ever get her memory back. Marcos answers me with a look. Then he starts playing some melodies on the guitar, looking into the fire. Will she ever get it back? When she remembers, what will she do? Will she gather us all together? Mariela doesn't know if she wanted to know. What if her memory comes back in ten years? She didn't want to know in ten years. Marcos doesn't know if he'd want to know, either. Then he asks if he can play a song for us.

Did he write it?

'I just wrote it,' he says, and when Mariela and I are silent, he asks if we want to hear it or not.

I look at him and listen to him and it's like being with Alejandro. You're like him, you sound like him, I told him.

'Should I play it for you or not?' he asks. 'I'll play it.'

Marcos doesn't know how to play the guitar. I mean: he plays better than I do, but I barely know seven chords. He's spent time practicing, he has plenty of fluidity in his left hand, but he isn't very good at following a rhythm, and you can tell from a mile off that he doesn't really know how to play. I've finished my first cigarette and I start to roll another to listen to Marcos's song, remembering that I too – with my seven chords – had come up with two or three songs of my own, not without pride but in secret.

Mariela goes to get a plastic chair and drags it over to the fire. It's hot. It must be twenty-four, twenty-five degrees out, and Marcos is sweating. No sooner does he start to play than we're startled by Dad's footsteps on the little gravel walkway.

'What's on your face?' cries Mariela, the first of us to see the blood.

Dad has scratch marks on one side of his face. The blood blurs the scratches, but we can see them more clearly when he draws closer to the light of the flames: three dark stripes from his cheekbone to his jaw. A fourth, much shorter, reaches the side of his nose.

'Did Mum do that to you? You didn't clean it or anything? You need to wash it out. You need to disinfect that,' Mariela is saying, as she tries to give him her plastic chair.

Dad goes on his own and grabs the lounge chair under the lemon tree at the end of the garden and hauls it over until he's beside me.

'You're bleeding, Dad,' says Mariela. 'You're dripping blood all over.'

There are drops of blood on Dad's white shirt and on the cushion of the lounge chair. Dad rubs at them without much interest and fixes the backrest so he won't be totally horizontal. He sits down.

'Bring me some water, Marita, will you?' he says. 'Were you going to play something, Marcos?'

'A song I wrote.'

'Play,' Dad tells him.

I remember asking him if he was going to tell us what had happened, and Marcos reaching to grab a roach he'd left on the front step of the lair, asking me for the lighter and lighting it. When Mariela brings the water, instead of drinking it, Dad pours a little onto his hand and rinses his wounds. He does this several times, then sets the glass on the ground. Turning down Mariela's offer to bring alcohol or iodine, he tells us that nothing happened.

'What had to happen happened. Your mother talked, I talked. She answered me, I answered her, she didn't like my answer. Mum wants to die. I don't. Mum thinks that I should want to die. But I don't want to die. Play, Marcos,' he says, but Mariela wants to know whether Mum had ended up with Ale's phone. She wants to know what Mum intends to do with Ale's phone.

'It doesn't matter,' I hear Dad say as I take a drag on the joint. 'She's the mother.'

'And what's that supposed to mean?' asks Mariela.

'Alejandro is her son.'

'Mum didn't know Alejandro,' she says. 'She always judged him, always criticised him, same as she does to all of us. We knew Alejandro.'

'She's still his mother,' says Dad, starting to get riled up. The bleeding is subsiding now; it's just a trickle.

'What's the point of being a mother if you don't know your son?' Mariela asks. 'Why isn't she here now, with us?'

'Parents know things about their children that not even their children know. Marcos, if you're going to play, play.'

Without thinking, I hand the joint to Dad and Dad takes it and asks what it is. Then he takes a puff and starts to cough. Marcos tells him to go easy and Dad takes another drag and tries to pass it to Mariela, but she refuses with a wave of her hand.

The song has lyrics but they're not finished, explains Marcos after he reaches to take the joint from Dad's hand and throws what's left into the fire. He's just going to hum the melody so we can get an idea of how it's turning out. It isn't bad. I light a cigarette and close my eyes, and after a couple of measures I thank God it's much better than I'd expected. Long and slow, strummed from start to finish, it evokes the highway, and it doesn't lose its charm even when Marcos slips up. I don't open my eyes while he plays, sitting there in front of the lair, the place where I'm going to live for the first four months after I separate from Brenda, hating myself for having no choice but to run to Mummy and Daddy's. At first I'll sleep in

Mariela's old room, but soon my parents' pity for me will become unbearable, especially in the evenings, when we all go to bed and a painful, unnatural silence will reign; it will end up driving me out to the lair to find solace with Alejandro. He's going to share his breakfasts with me and at night, after we have dinner with our parents, we'll shut ourselves in, him to compose songs or practice for the Music School admissions, me to write my first texts in ten years, stories about fathers and mothers and children and the cracks that open up between them, stories whose atmosphere will be impregnated with Leo Brouwer's *Estudios Sencillos*, with the marijuana and *grapamiel* that we're going to consume until I get sleepy. Ale will usually stay awake a little longer; when I throw a mattress on the floor, he goes up to the loft and plays on a little stool by the glow of a dim portable lamp, playing softly so I can sleep in peace, never complaining, happy to put up with me, sometimes even disappearing for days at a time, staying with some girl so I can have the place to myself. Dad sniffs and chews and swallows, but I don't open my eyes, not until Marcos finishes playing and I hear the logs shifting in the fire.

Marcos has the pile of firewood in reach. He's left the guitar on the floor to take another couple of logs from among the tangle of branches left after the pruning. Mariela picks up the guitar and leans it against the bars, saying that she doesn't know what the song has reminded her of, but she likes it. I relight my cigarette, which has gone out, and only then does Dad clear his throat.

'Don't you all feel like Alejandro is still here?' he asks. 'My tears are boiling hot. Do the dead ever really leave?'

'It's the scratches that are burning you,' Mariela tells him. 'Not the tears.'

'Thank you, marijuana,' says Marcos then. He's produced another joint from who knows where, and he lights it. 'Thank you, marijuana; thanks, weed; thanks reefer; thanks, ganja...'

'Thanks, doobie; thanks, grass...' Dad continues. His teeth are chattering, and Marcos brings him a fleece blanket. Dad wraps himself up until he's covered to the nose and his shoes are left sticking out. He kicks them off in two movements, without using his hands. He moves his toes inside the white socks, rubbing his feet, and little by little he stops shaking.

Before all of this, as soon as we'd returned from the funeral, I'd gone to the computer room − which had once been my room − intending to email Ricardo and tell him about Alejandro. Since he'd left for Barcelona we'd written to each other once or twice a year, always at critical moments. It shouldn't have surprised me at all to find an email from Ricardo already in my inbox. He'd sent it that very morning and it consisted of a single line: *How's things, Titan?* he asked me. But the fact that Ricardo had beat me to the punch only reinforced the euphoria I'd felt when I got back from the cemetery, and I wrote him about Ale and the lightning in one long, intense rant. Then, as a postscript, I told him about the dream I'd had about him, when I'd got into his flayed red car after leaving a party full of famous people.

The strange thing was that he answered me almost immediately. In his reply he said he was very sorry, and he sent me a big hug and another for my parents and siblings. Then he said: *Try not to turn him into a hero.*

I knew what he was trying to say. I listened to Ricardo when he talked, even if I didn't like what he had to tell me. I spent a good while staring at the screen.

During his last period in Montevideo he had set out to write an autobiographical novel that would exorcise every last one of his demons. He knew he was possessed. Artists were possessed or sick and their artworks were exercises in wallowing in their own shit, or half-hearted exorcisms. Half-hearted because artists were sick people who didn't want to be cured, because if they were cured they would no longer be artists. That was their greatest fear: that once they were cured they would have no reason to create. At least Nick Cave – Ricardo's hero – had said something like that in an interview. 'I'm sick, and the last thing I want is to get well.' Had Cave said it, or was it Mick Harvey, his eternal friend and guitar player, who'd said it about Cave? I thought Cave's attitude was the height of sanity, but Ricardo thought the opposite, and he's going to start his novel intending for it to be his last book, and it will be. He will never finish it. I don't remember if he abandons it at page fifty or sixty, but it's not long after that he exiles himself to Barcelona, where he will discover that his vocation is medicine, not writing, and he'll end up dedicating himself to Gestalt psychology.

In the way I'd written him about Alejandro's death, Ricardo must have caught traces of my euphoria or hints of literature. He must have thought I was assembling a story to protect myself from the pain. Although a lightning bolt wasn't psychological – although a lightning bolt was magical – he still made me suspect myself. Even when he was wrong, Ricardo was always a little bit right. Maybe the difference was that he now saw things like a therapist and I still saw them like a storyteller, the way a cave man would see them.

The next day, my birthday, we take Alejandro's ashes to La Paloma. These aren't like the fine dust left after burning firewood. They're grey, greenish grey, with gravelly lumps that disintegrate when you squeeze them. The black feather had gone with the coffin into the funeral parlour. Did they burn it with the body? The ashes aren't contained in a delicate urn, but rather in a square plastic receptacle, a kind of thick, grey taper that my father seals with duct tape before we go into the water so it won't open accidentally.

First, we gather on the sand. There are more than seventy of us. Family and friends have come from Montevideo, from Costa, from Maldonado, from Rocha. There are lifeguards from Zanja Honda and from Los Botes. It isn't an afternoon for the beach. The wind is blowing from the southeast and the sky is almost entirely covered with clouds. There is Agustina, who arrived after we'd already formed a circle. Her hair is very short and dyed blond and she has tattoos on her shoulders. She is no longer a pretty little thing. She's a woman.

Dad, the scratches on his face now a brownish yellow, starts out holding the urn. He says some words. He ends by proposing that we link arms with the people on either side of us and shout a motto of the Hawaiian lifeguards. One protects all, all protect one. Arms linked, we repeat it three times. Then it's Mum's turn to hold Alejandro's ashes. There are so many emotions running through her that her expression is one of shock. She says many things. What she says the most are these words: my son. When she's finished, Agustina walks to her, slowly and nervously, and reaches out her hands. Mum hesitates for a split second before handing her the urn.

Alejandro and Agustina had lost their virginity together, when he was sixteen and she fifteen. When she holds Alejandro's ashes in her hands, Agustina embraces them tenderly. Then she raises them up and turns in a complete circle, showing them to the clouds, the wind and all that sand that stretches all the way to the lagoon. We don't have a ritual. We don't know where we came from or where we're going, but while Agustina holds his ashes up toward some grand, nameless wellspring, Mum isn't Ale's mother. No one will be able to understand her pain, but while it lasts, Mum is her son's sister; though only for a second, we are all brothers and sisters.

More than twenty of us go into the water with our boards. There are small waves, under a metre in height. Heading out into the rip current, we go past the break and form a circle. Dad is in the middle. When he tries to pull the tape off the urn, he finds that he can't. He'd put it on too tight, and now it's wet. He looks nervous, and finally he gives up and brings the urn to his mouth to tear off the tape with his teeth, like a Neanderthal biting his new-born's umbilical cord.

I get quickly out of the water. I don't stick around to embarrass myself. Nor could I – I'm very out of shape, and the waves are no good either. It's been ten years since I've surfed: it was only a few kilometres away, at the mouth of the lagoon, where I'd herniated a disc. I could just stay there sitting on the board, remembering, but today the memories are hurtling toward me without my needing to summon them. During the whole drive to La Paloma with the ashes in the Fiat Premio, I had also been in the Ami 8, then in the Ford Falcon and the Belina, watching the countryside pass by, sensing the beach waiting for us, the salt in the air, the little cabin in Rincón del Rosario, the breath of the pines. We'd even stopped for a moment in front of the cabin, our cabin, which since the crisis of 2002 had passed into the hands of a widower, a carpenter by profession. In that little six-by-five metre cabin, we'd go to bed early, exhausted; it was so small it only had one room, though there was a loft where my parents and Mariela slept, and once the lights were out we'd start to talk. We'd go over the day and religiously review the waves and then, whatever it was we were talking about, we'd start to find it funny. In the darkness and the silence of the house, anything sounded comical, even the scritch-scratch of the shipworms eating away at the drywall. The sound of a voice in the darkness was extravagant, and often, when sleep was starting to overcome us, we couldn't tell who was talking. Then we weren't saying sentences anymore, just random words. Invented words, mispronounced words, fraying sounds. Dad and Mum would ask us to be quiet from their room, and sometimes we'd hear them laughing at the things we said and at our laughter, and a feeling of gratitude would descend over the cabin. And suddenly you'd realise it had been a long time since the last person spoke. You'd say something to sound out the atmosphere, and sometimes you'd get a half-muffled reply if you hadn't fallen totally, inadvertently asleep in the middle of it all, secured against any future darkness.

Aunt Laura comes out to meet me as soon as I touch the shore. For some reason she offers to help me with the board. The group that had stayed on land has moved further back, closer to the dunes. My aunt wishes me a happy birthday. She'd forgotten to say it before. Mum is staring out at the sea, her feet bare and wet. I look for Agustina. First I scour the beach with my eyes, then I ask after her. Someone who knows her saw her leave.

(There are twenty, maybe thirty of us who go into the water with our boards. There are small waves, under a metre high. We head out in the rip current past the break and form a circle, with Dad in the middle. When he tries to pull the tape off the urn, he finds that he'd pressed it on too tightly and it's wet, and finally he gives up and starts to bite it. Just when he gets the top open, an out-of-set wave rises up.

Waves reach the coast in ordered sets. Sets of three, sets of five, sets of seven. Then, when the set ends, there's a period of calm. Every once in a while, unpredictably, in that oasis, a wave appears that's much larger than the others. It can get to be twice as high as the set waves and so it breaks sooner; it usually catches the surfers by surprise, and they're forced to paddle out en masse so it won't break right on top of them. The sui generis wave that rears up exactly as my father opens the urn is nearly two metres high, and if it breaks, it's going to be practically impossible to keep the container steady in all the foam. The wave surges and curls as if it's going to break, but it doesn't. It's grey, it feints a couple of times, but then it grows fat and lifts us all up on its crest. Dad, no dummy, scatters the ashes into it.

When I come out of the water I notice that the group that stayed on land has moved back, toward the dunes. Aunt Laura comes straight over to meet me. The wave that Alejandro's ashes rode has passed the last water mark by more than twenty metres and everyone has had to run, rushing to pick up the bags and clothes off the ground to keep them from being soaked. The water got their feet wet.

'Your mother and I didn't move. It was Ale giving us his last hug. These are the things you talk about later on and no one believes you,' says my aunt.)

Agustina doesn't turn up at 8.30, when the lifeguards from Santa Teresa and Punta del Diablo arrive, plus the brigade from Rocha who knew Alejandro and hadn't been able to get out of their shifts for the funeral. I call her a couple of times. She answers the second call. She's still in La Paloma; she hasn't gone back to Montevideo. She's in a place that reminds her of Alejandro. I would have liked to be there with her. I want to be there with you, I say to her, but she doesn't want to tell me how to find her.

In under half an hour all the lifeguards are gathered, strong men who smell of sun, young men who've stopped somewhere on the way to buy bouquets of flowers. I know very few of them. Marcos and my old man know almost all of them. Canary and Dwarf are there. I stay close to them: they were the ones who'd found Alejandro in the lifeguard hut. He was dead, but they had tried to resuscitate him.

At a certain point I hear, from one little group, someone saying that Alejandro hadn't been a lifeguard. Lifesaver, yes, lifeguard, no.

'Alejandro didn't do any prevention. He liked to rescue people.'

The guy says it as a criticism, in a jealous tone of voice, accusing Ale of being irresponsible. One of the others finds the comment funny or worthy of celebration, and he laughs.

Later, when everyone is ready, they go into the water with their bouquets. They try to keep the flowers out of the water as they swim. Marcos dives in too. The sun is going down but it isn't a colourful sunset; it's metallic. They swim out in the strong rip tide, which drags and separates them.

There are countless things still to happen. For example, I still have to worry everyone by becoming skeletal so that I can try to tune in to Ale on his new wavelength. I still have to start talking out loud to him at night, asking him questions he never answers about this business of being dead, and I still, one day, have to let myself imagine his final moments inside the hut on Playa Grande. During the whole initial phase, I will forbid myself from picturing it: there was a reason why we couldn't find anything out about those moments, I tell myself. Ana Laura, the only witness, lost her memory, leaving Ale alone with his own death and leaving us with a perfect mystery. Any supposition makes me gnash my teeth. That he was afraid, that he tried to call someone on the phone, that he'd regretted going to the hut. It seems to me that people are trying to rob Alejandro of something sacred. His death was his and no one else's and I want them to leave it alone. But then, one stormy night, at home with Clara, I imagine it. The wind is blowing in from the southeast, and there's a lot of thunder and lightning and breaking of tree branches. Then the electricity goes out and during the remaining hours we spend awake, we use the light from the fire in the fireplace. The thunder is loud and sounds very near, and Clara is afraid. She's worried because she can't remember closing the windows of her house, and we start to make love partly to distract her. I'm down to skin and bones, I weigh seventy-five kilos. Clara is getting turned on, growing more and more demanding, and I start to get worked up and to lose my strength. She and Brenda are the only people who reproach me for my skinniness and encourage me to eat. Brenda asks me to think of my sons and I turn stubborn, telling myself: I am not going to eat for my children, I'm not going to turn them into my reason for living, I won't do that to them. She sees that my lungs are suffering and she says:

135

the Chinese interpret that as melancholy. Mum also lets me know, in her own way, that she isn't indifferent to my condition; my face gets ugly when I'm so skinny, she says. That night, after I collapse onto her back, Clara looks at me over her shoulder in the flashing lightning and the light from the fire. My heart is beating uncontrollably. I feel emaciated and haggard and I smell bad, like a dying man.

As my sperm perish in her armoured vagina, Clara massages me to prolong my pleasure. And I realise – it's so obvious now – that Ale had been afraid, and that at some point his eyes must have looked with sorrow at everything around him, just as mine are doing now. For a few moments, his gaze had passed over the peeling walls and ceiling of the lifeguard hut, making him remember all the winters it had survived, the care put into it by Dwarf and Canary, who lived in Punta del Diablo all year round and saw to repairing it and getting it into shape for the spring. That was when he recovered his faith and pictured himself basking in the morning sun, once the scare was over, the night transformed into an anecdote. He also must have thought about us, the way I'm now thinking about my children, my parents, my siblings. He must have experienced the same fetid emotions that all men feel at the hour of their death. I saw him with his little girlfriend, soothing her. I see them making love, him a sunny-pelted Viking, taking his last breath inside her as she goes crazy in the static-heavy air. As I think back on it now it seems naïve, but at one point I had my brother dancing and singing between thunderclaps. He sang a *ranchera* song that he'd improvised in the living room at my house, in front of the fireplace, one of the nights during the month or so he'd stayed with me after leaving the apartment in Montevideo. I told him, not totally serious, that it was his best song ever, and he hadn't liked that because he was just fooling around. The *ranchera* suddenly turns into a tango, then a rock song, finally into a waltz. *Free as a bird that flies in the night / just as it does in the day,* went the lyrics. *Free as a fish swimming in the Atlantic / just as it does the Pacific. A white sand / piper soaring over the plain,* sang Ale in my imagination. *Plane crashes down in the garden / Who could it have been? / Could it be Marilyn?* It was very likely that he'd picked up the guitar sometime during the night. It was almost impossible that he'd chosen that particular song, but I have all the freedom in the world, I can imagine it however I wanted, and I imagine him flinging his most spontaneous lyrics into the wall of sound that was closing around him. Then there's the film of his life, the one you supposedly see when you die. If Ale was anything, it was that incredible film, the reel that had taken thirty-one years to make so that only he could see it, and it's something I can't imagine. It was very likely too that if the girl had let him, Ale had fallen asleep, even if he felt the infinite pressure of the cosmos on his poor body. He had the gift of being able to fall asleep anywhere, in any position.

But the book ends here, on the night of his funeral, while Dad eats an apple beside the lounge chair and stretches his legs. Marcos, sweaty and shirtless, receives the heat from the fire on his hands. Mariela alternates between looking at the fire and looking toward the house. My feet are cramping up: when I take off the Adidas, I can feel the shape of the soles of his feet on my own. My muscles feel the pressure of his footprints in the trainers, which I've been walking on all day long.

Mariela is worried about Mum. She's worried that Mum has done something stupid. The house lights are all still on and not a sound can be heard. They needed to be turned off. Why didn't she go do that?

'Your mother isn't going to do anything,' Dad reassures her.

'She said she wanted to die.'

'She wouldn't be able to do something like that.'

Mariela – and this is one of those things that wouldn't work in a novel – is pregnant. She doesn't know it yet. It isn't a planned pregnancy. She'll find out one week later. She'll call to tell me in an ocean of tears. I'm going to ask her if it might finally be a little boy, and she'll say she doesn't care in the slightest. So, pregnant with a little boy whose organism is perfect, feeling without knowing it that she's standing before the gates of the mystery of restoration, Mariela says: 'Tomorrow I'll go and apologise to her.'

'Yes, better tomorrow. Better leave her alone now.'

During the night, Mum will answer two calls that come to Alejandro's mobile phone. Two women: one of them, from Marcos's group of friends, will tell her how Alejandro had saved her life. How one day she'd come by to see Marcos but instead she'd found Ale, who had offered her *mate* and had the patience to listen to her, and how afterwards he'd gone with her to the bus stop and there, with one of those hugs of his, wordlessly, he had dissuaded her from downing a blister pack of Lexotan. It will be the first of many nights that Mum sleeps with Ale's iPhone under her pillow. No one will ever be able to understand her pain.

Mum is also going to put photographs of Alejandro everywhere. On the fireplace mantel, her most beautiful baby is going to be depicted in a series interrupted only by the photo of Mariela and Milena, which still occupies the central spot.

'Good idea,' I'm going to say when she shows them to me the next day, although my reason tells me otherwise.

What are we going to do with Alejandro's death? Are

we going to let it leave us the same as we'd been before? What would he have wanted? What is family for?

At three o'clock, my phone rings. Dad is asleep on the lounge chair, Marcos is smoking. For some reason, Mariela thinks it's Mum calling and she follows me along the little gravel path to eavesdrop on our conversation. I have to tell her and tell her again that it was a personal call, and to leave me alone and go back to the fire.

'Is it Brenda?' she asks.

'Be smart,' she tells me then, before heading back to the lair.

It's strange that she would say that to me. Mariela doesn't know anything about what these recent weeks have been like between Brenda and me. At any rate, I haven't talked about it with her. Maybe Alejandro had told her something. In any case, her advice reverberates in me. Mariela had been the only one, during my crisis at nineteen, who had come to me to say it hurt her to see me so sad. The only one who had cried with me. Be smart. Be smart.

Alejandro's death is like the death of something that died in a forest or a garden. A leaf, a fallen branch, a bird. It would be food for other trees, other creatures: it was what couldn't cease to happen. That's what I'm thinking about when I answer.

Brenda is calling to tell me that she couldn't sleep. I stay silent when she says it. In that moment, a memory arises. It's the memory of the first and only weekend we'd spent together at La Paloma. That weekend, not even a month after we'd met, we had decided that we were going to move in together and that we would have children. But we didn't decide it, we didn't reason; we knew. We had come together for that. It was something almost impersonal; nature had brought us together to make more life. I said to her: hopefully they'll have your eyes. I looked inside her eyes when we were coupling. Something within them invoked something in mine, and what was in mine came out to meet what was in hers. I knew that what came from behind her eyes and mine was going to give our children their form, as much or more than our gametes.

The fat guy woke her up with his snoring and she can't get back to sleep, Brenda says, as I walk between two worlds and watch the butterflies flying around us. I've never seen butterflies in Los Botes. And it wasn't just one butterfly, or two: there were dozens of them fluttering in the sunlight. Brenda doesn't like the beach. She doesn't like displaying herself in public and she doesn't like the waves, but it was March and La Paloma was empty. The water was placid as a lake, very blue, and she had put on a denim miniskirt and some coloured sandals with rubber soles, wedges, to go down to the beach. She and I. She walked with her rubber soles along the dirt roads, and then on the shifting sand. And suddenly, when we were embracing and she had wrapped her legs around me, the butterflies: the fucking universe giving us its blessing.

I'm in the garage. My voice echoes. I don't want to talk too much until I'm out in the street. My parents' house is completely silent and Mum will surely be able to hear me. Be smart.

'I wake up every night,' she's saying. 'I sit looking at him. The gut on him. I swear to you, I look at him and sometimes I can't understand what I'm doing with this guy.'

Once I'm walking on the pavement, I think about how Brenda is only a few blocks away. There couldn't have been more than five hundred metres between us. Five hundred steps. Two, three minutes. She's still talking about Fabricio. She's saying that she doesn't know what it is they have together, but that there was affection. Obviously, it went beyond the physical. In a way, they were like brother and sister. Siblings, or friends. It was something totally new for her. I almost remind her that she had already said this to me. She speaks quietly. I picture her sitting in bed beside Fatman. When I finally open my mouth, it's to tell her that I've been thinking about the butterflies. That makes her stop talking. That's all I say, butterflies. I don't have to add anything else. Butterflies, for us, means that moment in Los Botes. Who was going to believe that one morning there were butterflies on the beach, flying over the surface of the Atlantic while a man and a woman made love? Who was going to believe it, and who would care?

'That was beautiful,' she says. 'That was romantic. That was a little piece of glory. It was all like that with you in the beginning.'

None of this should matter to me the night of my brother's funeral. Supposedly Alejandro's death has put everything into perspective, but I can't control myself. I tell her that it would always be a little piece of glory and she, as if she had prepared it, replies that it was a shame one couldn't live in those little pieces of glory forever.

Then there is silence. Brenda is taking sips from a cup of tea, or smoking. I could go on walking all night, listening to that silence, but eventually she speaks again. She says that was the thing about romanticism: it ends, it lasts no time at all. I reply that I hadn't put those butter-flies there. Neither had she. No one had put them there. It hadn't been romantic.

It was real, I tell her. Brenda says that romantic love isn't love.

141

'People can kill with that kind of love,' she says.

Then I had never loved her. I think I even say it aloud, but Brenda isn't listening to me; she goes on as if I'd said nothing.

'When you left I felt a ripping here, in my belly. As if something had been torn out by the root. I couldn't stop crying. I spent days, weeks crying. I didn't know what was happening to me. What we had was special. It's not something that happens to everyone. I don't know what I'm doing with this guy. He's fat, he snores at night, but he's good, and I'm not afraid with him. I'm afraid of going from one man to another my whole life,' she says.

By then I'm already standing in front of her house.

The house has two floors. The only tree in the front garden is a tall old palm tree. Brenda had invited me in the first time I'd brought the boys over, around the middle of January. I should have stayed outside, but the owner of the house wasn't there and she wanted to show me the kids' rooms in the loft. Now they would each have their own room, and they were large and looked out over the back garden. On the way to the kitchen, where she would offer me a *mate*, she pointed to the master bedroom on the first floor. Behind the closed door she'd set up a consulting room. I look at it all confusedly and I manage to notice, through the kitchen window, the shadow of an arbour and a small above-ground pool, four by two metres. On one of the surrounding walls they'd built an additional room for Yamila to sleep in.

The light in the living room, which looks out to the street, is on. There, Brenda is drinking her tea, sitting at the table with the phone to her ear. When I tell her I can see her from the street, she comes to the window. Then she crosses the room and opens the front door, barefoot, in tracksuit bottoms and a t-shirt. Let me in, I tell her. We're going to talk.

Seeing that this is serious, she leads me by the hand into the kitchen, asking me how we all are, adjusting her braids. She puts water on to boil and crosses her arms. For several moments, Fabricio's snores are the only sound. We're going to talk about what we were talking about, I'm about to say, but she gets ahead of me. Uncrossing her arms, she tells that she's open to having relations with me.

She says it in these words: 'Dani, I'm open to having relations with you. I've been thinking about it and it's what I want.'

She says it to my face. Apparently she'd talked to Fabricio that very afternoon. To Fabricio, I learn, it seems like the most natural thing in the world for Brenda to want to have relations with the father of her children. If he could choose, he would choose that she only have relations with him, but if that's what she needs, he thinks the worst thing Brenda can do is repress it.

'The desire is still there,' she says, breathing deeply. 'I can't deny it.'

Fabricio is a good man. Simple, not too bright, but a good man, says Brenda, and my heart freezes and a shell covers me in a head-to-toe layer of steel. I can't manage an answer, but her eyes widen as if I'd said something barbaric when I grab her by the throat. Brenda grasps hold of my forearms, she says my name. There's not much air passing through her trachea. I can feel Mariela in the back of my head as if she'd followed me the whole way there, as if she were standing right behind me. I want to tear Brenda's head off. I know I'm not going to kill her, but I think: *if I kill her I'm free,* and I squeeze a little

143

harder. Her eyes don't know what they're looking at. Then I picture myself entering her there, in her new kitchen, with the fat man's snores in the background. I'd sit her on the wooden counter, take off her trousers, and enter her. In that position I always used to feel like I reached her belly button. Something that isn't pleasure or pain would force her to grab herself there, just above her waist. I'd always stop when her eyes filled with tears. Brenda would always tell me to keep going. And I'd keep going, admiring and jealous of that inexplicable thing she was feeling. A couple of times no. A couple of times she'd been the one to ask me to stop, and I always stopped and asked questions.

What a mess it would be, I tell her when I let her go.

As we're catching our breath, I tell her that I'm going to take the boys for a walk. I'm agitated, too. Brenda doesn't seem like she's going to return my aggression, and I ask her to help me wake them up and dress them. It doesn't provoke any suspicion in me that she doesn't put up much resistance; she only grabs me by the arm as we leave the kitchen and says to wait, it's still dark.

Just a little while, I tell her. Then I'll bring them back to you. I promise her.

Though the heat hasn't let up, we put trainers and tracksuits on them. Paco gets up quickly. He reaches out his arms to me as soon as he opens his eyes, and he's excited even though he doesn't understand what's happening. Juan flops backward onto the bed as his mother dresses him. We lead him down the stairs by the hand, and only after drinking a glass of water does he wake up a little. He asks where we're going. He's very sleepy.

'On a walk,' said Paco, repeating my words. 'It's just for a little while.'

The sky is still scored with violet clouds. The dogs,

when they hear us, start to bark. I lead them toward the beach along Ecuador, the street where our house is. Did they know that I'd been a child in that neighbourhood? Now they were going to be children in the same place where I'd been a boy.

I hold them by the hand at first, and they listen; they seem attentive. On the way to the beach there are four houses that Grandpa Miguel used to say belonged to the three little pigs and the big bad wolf. They're still there. I point them out to the boys. We used to believe the whole story. The houses grew in size. The last one, the wolf's, was gigantic and abandoned and always gave us the creeps. It was across from the beach, and it was a three-floor mansion with a very steep, gabled roof; it was always dark, dilapidated, the garden overgrown. It had recovered some splendour much later, when it had been turned into an experimental elementary school. Now it's been abandoned again and smothered with weeds. At this early hour of the morning, it's a terrifying sight. One of them whispers: 'The wolf's house.'

Crossing Parque Avenue, I show them the spot where I'd thrown my first punch. I'd been walking with Ale and Federico, my best friend. I was twelve, Alejandro six. We'd run an errand at El Grillito, a better-stocked shop than the one we had on the corner by our house. Alejandro was picking up pebbles as we walked. When the boys and I reach the exact place, we stop.

There, on the other side of the street, there will be a skinny kid and his friend. Out of nowhere he comes over and starts to shove me, I tell them. He's going to shove me and he's going to say that Ale is picking up pebbles to throw at them. I'll tell him that no, it's nothing like that, he's playing, he's my kid brother, he's little, he's collecting them. But the boy insists, insists, he will say that I told my brother to gather the stones so we could throw them at him. And I'll swear up and down that it never even occurred to me. Suddenly my arm shoots out and lands on his head, on his ear, and the kid is laid out there in the street, almost on the curb. Then, when he gets up, he starts yelling at us, but now he doesn't have the nerve to approach us, and we leave.

'What did that kid's friend do?' asks Juan.

The friend didn't want anything to do with it, I don't think. He watched it all and laughed. Do you know what we called the skinny bully after that? Pebble-breaker. I don't know why. But every time we passed by his house, we said: there's Pebble-breaker's house. But maybe he didn't even live there, because I never saw him again.

Paco and Juan keep up with me. They're used to walking. Back when we'd lived in Villa Argentina with their mother, before we bought the car, we used to walk everywhere. To the beach, to the Tienda Inglesa on Atlántida. Sometimes I'd forget myself and walk at my normal pace, but they never complained. They'd take their fast little steps, and on walks of twenty or thirty blocks we'd only sit down once or twice to rest in the shade.

Going down along San Francisco, we come out onto the plaza with the Strawberry. The Strawberry was a cedar tree over six metres high, a tall fat cedar that had been shaped like an upside-down strawberry. It wasn't anymore. It had lost all its foliage. The branches on one whole side had disappeared after a storm, or maybe the tree had already started to dry out. The branches of the Strawberry were so perfect and compact that we'd been able to climb up to the top, then sit on the branches and slide down. The boughs were flexible, and the last ones stopped a metre from the ground. We walk under the Strawberry's broken dome, and Paco and Juan look up and admire it. They picture us, me and my siblings, going down the world's longest slide.

Alejandro is going to break his arm here. Instead of sliding half lying down, he wanted to do it sitting up as straight as possible, and at the bottom he's going to go flying head first. Luckily he's going to put his arm out, because if he'd fallen on his head, he would have cracked it open. I remembered Ale wearing a cast that went almost up to his shoulder. It was going to itch, and he was sometimes going to be proud of it.

Paco is an intelligent boy, a sharp boy. He asks why I'm talking funny.

'Why are you talking like everything's in the future?' he asks me. 'All that stuff already happened.'

Then I think of Brenda. I imagine that I'd really strangled her and that now she's dead in the kitchen of her house, and I'm filled with emotion. For a second, I think I hear sirens. No sooner had we left than Brenda called the police to report that I'd kidnapped the boys. She had never seen me like that. I had never exploded. I can feel the bite of her fingers on my forearm.

Then Juan says: 'Uncle Ale went to heaven.'

After he says it, he makes a sound, boohoo, pretending to sob. It gives me a strange feeling, then I find it funny. The two of them start to run around the tree; they go up to the trunk and touch it, reaching their arms up, but the bottom branches are too high for them.

The sirens are getting closer; I can hear them clearly now. I can see the lights of the police car spinning above the roofs of the houses. Shangrilá is beautiful at night, so still. The trees and the houses blend together and the sky looks like it does in the countryside. When the boys see the lights of the police car and hear the noise getting closer, they come to stand beside me. They are children of a murderous love. That's why they strong and healthy and full of energy. If they give me grandchildren someday, I hope they'll come from a love like that. Don't be scared, I tell them. Then Paco asks me if I'd cried a lot for Uncle Ale. Not yet, I reply.

'I would cry if you died,' he says. 'I'd cry if Juan died.'

'I'm not going to die,' says Juan.

'Everyone dies,' declares Paco.

'Not me,' replies Juan. Then he asks me if I'm crying.

I'm not crying. I have tears in my eyes but I'm not crying. Juan also has tears in his eyes, real ones now. I ask him if he's ever seen me cry.

'I saw Dad crying,' says Paco. Then he asks me when I'm going to cry for Uncle Ale.

I didn't want to cry two of the same tears. I wanted every tear to be worth something. I was going to write about that.

CHARCO PRESS

Director & Editor: Carolina Orloff
Director: Samuel McDowell

www.charcopress.com

Older Brother was published on
80gsm Munken Premium Cream paper.

The text was designed using Bembo 11.5 and ITC Galliard.

Printed in January 2020 by TJ International
Padstow, Cornwall, PL28 8RW

Printed using responsibly sourced paper and environmentally
friendly adhesive.